A SUMMER OF SECRETS

KAY CORRELL

ROSE QUARTZ PRESS

Published by Rose Quartz Press

This book is dedicated to Gloria…

story between series - with Josephine and Paul from The Letter.)

LIGHTHOUSE POINT ~ THE SERIES

Wish Upon a Shell - Book One
Wedding on the Beach - Book Two
Love at the Lighthouse - Book Three
Cottage near the Point - Book Four
Return to the Island - Book Five
Bungalow by the Bay - Book Six

SWEET RIVER ~ THE SERIES

A Dream to Believe in - Book One
A Memory to Cherish - Book Two
A Song to Remember - Book Three
A Time to Forgive - Book Four
A Summer of Secrets - Book Five

INDIGO BAY ~ A multi-author sweet romance series

Sweet Sunrise - Book Three
Sweet Holiday Memories - A short holiday story
Sweet Starlight - Book Nine

Sign up for my newsletter at my website *kaycorrell.com* to make sure you don't miss any new releases or sales.

CHAPTER 1

Cece Stuart pulled up in front of their family cabin on Lone Elk Lake and turned off her small sensible—and thankfully paid off—car. The drive to Sweet River Falls had seemed endless as she dodged large SUVs through the Friday night Denver traffic. It hadn't been much better after leaving the city. It seemed like half the Denver population had decided this weekend was a good one to head to the mountains.

And it was.

They were enjoying deliciously mild spring weather. Though she knew that could change in an instant and a late spring snowstorm could still hit the area.

She slid out of the car and gazed up at the

starlit sky above the lake. She sucked in the fresh air and stretched her arms wide. This, *this* was perfect. She loved this cabin, the lake, the town. She was grateful she and her sisters had worked out a way to keep the cabin in the family instead of selling it after their parents had died.

The door to the cabin opened and her sister Bree waved to her. "Come on in. I just got back from the lodge. I finished up all the food I could for catering tomorrow's wedding."

Cece grabbed her overnight bag, a duffel, and a large tote bag, and headed into the cabin. She dropped the bags as she entered and reached behind her to tug the door closed and broke into laughter. "Hey, you fixed the door. It doesn't fight you anymore."

"Jason fixed it. I actually tumbled through the door trying to hip check it open this week and landed on my rear. That was it. Jason came over and fixed it the next day." Bree laughed. "Only took us, what? Seven months or so to get it done?"

"That Jason of yours is a keeper."

"He is." Bree glanced down at her engagement ring.

Cece picked up her bags again and Bree eyed the load. "You got a lot of stuff there."

"I thought I'd leave some things here at the cabin since I seem to be coming here almost every weekend to help you out. This is the third weekend in a row."

"I know. And I appreciate it. The business really took off. I thought I'd just be doing the catering business, but somehow I've ended up being a semi-wedding planner, too, for Nora and Jason at the lodge. I really appreciate you helping with the planning side of things. I'm so overwhelmed."

"I enjoy it. Beats the heck out of my boring day job."

"You're so organized and the brides love talking to you. I set up two appointments tomorrow morning with brides. One is local, one is over Skype. She wants to have a destination wedding here, and she wants it by the end of the summer. Don't know how we'll make that happen. I'm booking up quickly."

"When do they think they'll have the new venue at the lodge finished?"

"They're hoping to have it finished by the end of June. They've already booked it out for weddings starting in July and a small company retreat in September. But the brides know there is a chance it won't be completely finished by then."

"That's really going quickly."

"They were lucky we had a milder winter. Supposed to be roofing it next week, I think. They have the back kitchen area started and all the ordered ovens, stove, and refrigerator are at the lodge in storage, just waiting to be installed. It will be nice to have a separate area to use for catering besides sharing the lodge's dining hall kitchen." Bree grabbed one of her bags. "Let me help."

They went to the bedroom that had been their sister Abby's room. Though Cece didn't know why they still called it Abby's room. Abby hadn't been here in months, and Cece used it every time she came to help out Bree. She felt a little bit like a nomad with the back and forth from Denver to Sweet River Falls each week, but she did enjoy helping her sister.

They dumped the bags on the bed. "Let me unpack and I'll come out and you can tell me about the two brides I'm talking with tomorrow and let me know what I can do to help with the wedding."

"Sounds good." Bree turned to leave, then

paused. "And really, Cece, thanks. I couldn't do this without you."

"Well, you took a leap of faith to move here and start your business over again. I encouraged you. It's not like I could let you flounder by yourself." She smiled at her sister, so glad they'd found their way back to being friends after years of being estranged.

"Well, you're the best. Not to mention the most organized person I know. Big help."

"Keep talking, you're great for my ego." Cece unzipped the duffle and tugged out some jeans and sweaters along with the black slacks and white shirt she wore when she helped cater the weddings. Exhaustion crept over her, but she determinedly unpacked every last thing and went to go join Bree for a rundown on the weekend ahead of them.

ZACH BERRY FROWNED as he clicked off his phone. Another delay. This building at the lodge was going to be the death of him. As much as it pained him to think it, he did miss having a business partner. It was so hard to juggle the business alone.

Not that he'd ever speak to his old partner again. He didn't talk to cheaters. If a man couldn't trust his business partner, there was no use in having one. He slid his phone into his jeans pocket and looked up at the starlit sky through the overhead beams. He was determined to get the venue under roof by the end of this coming week.

If it killed him.

Which, at this rate, it might.

He turned around at the sound of Jason Cassidy walking into the structure. "Looks like it's coming along great." Jason looked around the building.

Yeah, just great.

But he wasn't going to bog Jason down with the details.

It was his own job to get this project completed. And completed on time.

"It's coming along fine." He didn't consider that a lie, just that it was going to take a bit more finagling to get it done on time, and he was going to have to put in some very long hours. But then, he always put in long hours these days. It kept him busy and kept him from dwelling on…

Well, he wasn't going to think about that.

"Mom booked another family reunion for November. They're really excited about having this new building to use. I guess it's the grandparents' fiftieth wedding anniversary and family from all over the country is coming in for it. They booked up every empty cabin we had."

"I think this will be a great addition to Sweet River Lodge. You can have retreats, reunions, meetings. It was a solid business decision."

"Thanks. I'm hoping so. I've sunk a lot of our resources into it."

He knew Jason and his mother had a full schedule planned for the building once he could get it finished. They had the backup of using the lodge's main room off the dining hall, but it wasn't ideal for anything except small weddings.

If only his suppliers would quit their delays.

And his workers would quit having babies. He grinned at that one, remembering how excited Billy had been when he'd gotten the call his wife had gone into labor. The kid was only twenty-three and one of the most skilled carpenters he'd ever hired. But that pesky baby had decided to come early, and he'd given Billy the week off.

Hence the reason he was still here late on a Friday tonight, swinging a hammer.

"Mom wanted you to come to the lodge and get some dinner. You know she thinks you're starving out here."

He looked around the building and up at the stars taunting him through the as yet uncovered roof. Exhaustion overtook him and he set down his hammer. "You know what? I'll take you up on that offer. I am starving, and anything I'd rustle up at home would never be as good as the food at the lodge."

He followed Jason outside and down the pathway beside the lake. This really was going to be a nice looking wedding venue when it got finished. The Sweet River Lodge already did weddings outside during the summer but had no place to hold them if the weather turned ugly. This new venue would really open up their options. He wasn't surprised that Jason and his mother, Nora, had already booked up most of the weekends into the fall months along with a Christmas wedding.

But their first wedding was booked for the first of July. Which was going to be his deadline to meet no matter what. He wasn't about to go disappointing any brides. He was certain that would be bad karma.

CHAPTER 2

The next day Nora helped Cece and Bree with the last-minute preparations for the wedding. At lunchtime, she insisted the sisters sit down and have a bite to eat. No going hungry on her watch.

As the girls finished, she made up a lunch for Zach. She knew he wouldn't stop his work and come to the lodge, so she'd gotten into the habit of sending a lunch over for him. She packed it all in a basket and turned to Cece.

"Cece, would you mind running this lunch over to Zach at the new building?"

"Have you decided what you're going to call it?" Bree asked.

"I'm still trying on names. The Wedding Lodge seems a bit redundant with the whole resort being called Sweet River Lodge. Plus, we want to use it for more than just weddings."

"It sort of looks like a chalet with its high roofline and the rafters inside. You could call it The Chalet at the Lodge," Bree suggested.

Nora paused. "That's not a bad suggestion. Better than anything I've come up with so far."

"I really like the plan you came up with for it," Bree said.

"It wasn't me. It was Jason. He sorted through a bunch of wedding magazines looking at venues and did online searches until he and Zach came up with this design."

"Somehow I can't picture Jason browsing through wedding magazines." Cece smiled.

"My son will do anything to get the job done." Nora picked up the basket with Zach's lunch. "So you'll take it over to him?"

"Sure, no problem." Cece got up and took the basket. "I'll be back in a few to help you, Bree." She disappeared out of the kitchen.

Bree turned to Nora and grinned. "So, you sent her over with lunch because you wanted her to meet Zach, didn't you?"

"I figure there's no reason the two of them shouldn't meet. It's high time that girl found herself a good man, and Zach is about as good as they come."

Bree smiled again. "Always the matchmaker, huh?"

"It worked out well for you and Jason, didn't it?" Nora raised an eyebrow.

Bree laughed and reached for the mixing bowl in front of her. "Yes, you're right. It did."

CECE HEADED over to the new wedding lodge—building-chalet-whatever. The sun sparkled on the lake as she walked along the pathway. A beautiful day for the wedding. Jason had set up an arbor by the lake in front of the dining hall and was busy setting up chairs for this evening's wedding. Just last weekend she'd gotten twinkle lights for the arbor and simple lanterns to put at the end of each aisle of chairs. Nora had loved the tiny updates she'd made to their outside wedding setup and asked for more suggestions. She loved helping her out.

She waved to Jason when he looked up and saw her. He lifted a hand in answer and went back to setting up the seats. Good thing the weather was holding out because she'd seen the final guest count. It seemed the wedding had grown since they'd first talked about it, and there was no way all the guests would fit in the big great room of the lodge if bad weather had hit.

But the bride was lucky today. Nice weather and a pretty sunset as a bonus.

She entered the large structure at the far end of the property. The outside was rough pine logs and huge rafters vaulted above, ready for the roof. Large openings in the sides were for what she assumed would be massive picture windows overlooking the lake.

As she walked farther into the building, she spotted a man working alone in the sunshine that filtered down through the open roof. He'd taken off his shirt and the sun shone on his bare shoulders and ripped abs.

Not that she noticed them.

Much.

She stood and let him finish running his circular saw. She didn't want to startle him and cause an accident. Her father had taught her a lot about safety with power tools as he worked on his numerous projects around the cabin. The man—she assumed he was Zach—switched off the saw.

She called out to him. "Zach?"

He spun around as she approached. "Yes?"

"Hi. Nora sent me over with a picnic lunch for you."

He grabbed his shirt hanging on a nail beside him and unfortunately shrugged into it and buttoned a few buttons. So much for the view. "Nora thinks that I'm a starving bachelor." He gave her a rueful grin. "She feeds me all the time."

She didn't miss the word bachelor. She shook her head. Nora had deliberately chosen *her* to bring over the basket. "If it's anything like the lunch she made for my sister and me, you're in for a treat. Hope you got a slice of the apple pie, too. It was delicious." She held out the basket.

He wiped his hands on his jeans, took the basket, and peeked inside. "Looks like I did score a piece of her pie. Excellent. I'm pretty sure no one makes a pie better than Nora."

"I agree with you on that... and that's saying something because I think my sister is about the best cook in the world. Have you met her? Bree. She's doing catering for the lodge."

"I have. She's engaged to Jason, right?"

"She is. I've got to talk her into setting a

wedding date. She's been so busy starting up her business here that she keeps avoiding making a decision on the date."

"I guess they'll get married here in this new building?"

"I'm sure they will." Cece grinned. "If you put a roof on it."

The corners of his mouth turned up in a wry smile. "I'm working on it."

"Or if she doesn't book it up solid before she puts her own name on the list." She knew she was rambling, but something about this man caught her off guard.

He reached out a hand. "I'm Zach, by the way, though I guess you figured that out by now."

She slipped her hand in his, at once surrounded by rough skin and a firm handshake. "I'm Cece. Bree's sister."

"Nice to meet you. Cece, huh?"

"Short for Celeste, but the only one who ever called me that was my mother when I did something wrong."

"I'll keep that in mind." His lazy grin teased her.

She looked down to see that he still held her hand. He must have noticed at the same time because he set it free. Her hand immediately felt lonely and cold.

That was a silly thought, wasn't it?

Another silly thought—she wanted to invite herself to join him while he ate his lunch. But that would be strange to ask if she could join him because she'd already eaten, and she really needed to get back and help Bree. What would she say? Hi, can I sit and watch you eat?

She slipped her hand into her jeans pocket. "Well, I better go. Enjoy your lunch."

"I'm sure I will. Thanks for bringing it over to me." His smile said thanks, but something about his face held a depth of standoffishness.

Okay then, maybe she didn't want to stay after all. "You're welcome. It was no big deal. It's a pretty day for a walk."

"Yep."

Ugh, small talk.

"Okay, see you." She fled the structure before she could say one more meaningless comment.

ZACH WATCHED the cute brunette scurry away. He couldn't help but think that "scurry" was the exact right word to describe it. Like she couldn't wait to get away from him. But that was okay. He didn't need any entanglements while this project was taking up all his time.

Even if she did have the most interesting brown eyes with hints of golden sparkles in them. Even if she had a quick smile and a dimple on her left cheek. She had her hair pulled back in one of those complicated looking braid thingies that women wore. She was shorter than him, he'd guess only about five foot two or so. She'd barely come up to his shoulders.

And why had he noticed all these details?

But none of that mattered, of course. He'd sworn off women. That was the only logical thing to do after what happened with…

Nope, he'd also sworn that he wouldn't think about her. Wouldn't even allow himself to *think* her name.

He settled down on a sawhorse and pulled out a thick sandwich on homemade bread. Man, no other job was ever going to be as good as this one with meals like the ones Nora made for him.

Even if this job was trying to kill him.

CHAPTER 3

Cece sank onto the swing by the lake after returning to the cabin late that night following the wedding. She gratefully took the glass of wine Bree held out to her. "Thanks."

"That was a long one, wasn't it?" Bree dropped a blanket on Cece's lap.

"It was. I don't know how you do it. I'm exhausted."

"I'm thinking I'm going to need to hire some more help. And I don't know how I got wrapped up in doing so much of the wedding planning, too. I want to cook. I want to cater." Bree settled beside her, and Cece covered her sister's lap with half of the blanket.

"You know what?" Bree pushed off lightly

with her foot and started the swing in a gentle motion.

"What?" She took a sip of her wine and looked up at the starlit sky.

"I think you should consider moving to Sweet River Falls, too."

"What?" She swiveled her head and stared at her sister.

"Seriously. You could do the wedding planner side of the business. I could do the catering. There isn't another wedding planner here. It would be the perfect job for you. You're always saying that your day job is so boring."

She frowned. "It is. But... move here? Where would I live?"

"At the cabin, of course."

"With you?"

Bree laughed softly. "Of course with me. The past is behind us, Cece. I'm serious about this offer."

"You think we could grow the business enough to support both of us?"

"At the rate it's growing, we could support both of us *and* hire some help."

"But where are you and Jason going to live when you get married? I don't want to get in your way."

"We haven't really talked about that yet." Bree sighed. "I know we need to. We need to make wedding plans. Pick a date. I've just been so busy and Jason has been patient with me. And he's crazy busy himself. But I do want you to move here. If you want to."

"You want to hire me to work for you…" Cece still couldn't wrap her mind around the offer.

"No, actually…" Bree paused and took a sip of her wine. "I was thinking more like you'd be my partner. You run the planning side, I'll do the catering. But we could also back each other up."

"I…" Her pulse raced as she thought of the possibilities. Own part of her own business. Be her own boss or at least co-boss. Leave her dead-end job she hated going back to each Monday.

"You can think about it if you want. But I'd really, *really* love to have you. We work well together, don't we? And you charmed those brides you talked to today. You basically have both their weddings planned. You're great at that."

"I should probably think about it, you're right." A slow grin spread across her face.

Bree laughed. "But you've already made a decision, right?"

"I have. I'm going to turn in my notice on Monday."

"Atta girl. This is going to be great."

She frowned. "I'll have to deal with my place in Denver and all my stuff."

"Why don't you arrange to put your things in storage until we get everything sorted out? I ended up selling most of my things in Austin when I moved here. It was kind of... freeing."

"Freeing sounds good. Maybe I'll see about selling what I can of my things in Denver."

Her mind was reeling with a mental checklist of to-dos. "I better tell Petey, too."

"You mean Pete." Bree grinned.

"That. I'm having a hard time calling my son Pete after eighteen years of Petey."

So many changes in such a short time. Bree was once again her friend as well as her sister. Pete and Bree's son, Cody, were set to be roommates at Mountain View College this fall, and now it appeared she was moving to Sweet River Falls.

In spite of all the changes and all she now had to do with a move, a comforting feeling of rightness settled over her. She was coming home to where she belonged.

THE NEXT MORNING Cece and Bree headed back over to the lodge for breakfast. Jason walked up to them, a warm smile on his face, as they entered the dining hall. He pressed a quick kiss on Bree's forehead. "Well, this is a surprise."

"We were out of coffee and neither one of us felt like cooking." Cece shrugged.

"And I have news." Bree slipped her hand in Jason's.

"I can tell. I can read your face like a book. Spill it."

"Cece is moving here to Sweet River Falls." Bree's voice danced with excitement.

"No kidding. That's great." He turned to her. "What made you decide to move here?"

"Bree's offer to join her in her business."

"I think that's a *great* idea. Bree's been overwhelmed with everything since moving here. If you help her… maybe she'll have more time for me." Jason's eyes twinkled.

"And maybe she'll decide to set a wedding date." Cece eyed her sister.

"Hey, no ganging up on me. I'll set one. Soon."

"Can't be too soon for me." Jason squeezed Bree's hand.

"What's all the excitement over here?" Nora walked up to them.

"Cece's moving to Sweet River Falls and joining Bree in her business."

"That's great news." Nora nodded. "Bree can use the help. She's running herself ragged."

"Says the woman who never takes a day off." Bree gave Nora a wry smile.

"There is that." Nora grinned and turned to Cece. "So when are you moving?"

"I need to turn in notice to my company. Four weeks, I think. I don't want to leave them hanging."

"Perfect. You'll be here this summer for the busy season."

Everything was moving so quickly, but Cece felt like she'd made the right decision. She loved Sweet River Falls and was super excited about owning part of the business. Four weeks would give her time to get used to the idea, wouldn't it?

"Having a party here?"

She turned at the deep tones of Zach's voice and the heat of a blush crossed her cheeks.

What was up with that?

"Just found out that Cece is moving here to town." Jason nodded his head toward her.

"Oh."

Cece was strangely disappointed that there was not a hint of excitement in Zach's tone. Her move obviously meant nothing to him. But why should it? She'd just met him yesterday for mere moments.

She should quit acting like a high school girl with a crush.

Her mouth almost dropped open with the thought. She was acting like she had an instant *crush* on him. That was ridiculous.

She turned away from him.

Nora stepped closer to her. "So, you'll be helping with the wedding planning? I'd like to hire you to do all the wedding planning here at the lodge, and, of course, you'd be free to do planning at other places in town."

"That sounds fabulous. Yes. That's great."

"You don't even want to talk money?" Zach interrupted.

"I'm sure whatever Nora thinks is fair will work for me." She didn't know why Zach ruffled her nerves, but he did. Was he criticizing the first business decision she'd made?

"We'll iron out the details. I'm excited that you're moving here." Nora motioned to a table in the corner. "Come on, the lot of you, let's go sit down and have a nice big breakfast."

They all headed over to the table Nora kept open for friends and family who stopped by. Cece slipped into a seat next to Bree, and to her dismay, Zach sat down on the other side of her. Their shoulders bumped and the faint scent of a woodsy aftershave and fresh air surrounded her.

She pushed her hair away from her face and concentrated on the mug of coffee the waitress set in front of her.

And concentrated on it some more.

"You reading tea leaves in that coffee or something?" Zach's low voice whispered against her ear.

"I—no—" The warmth of a blush flushed her cheeks *again*. "I'm just trying to decide what to order." That sounded lame, even to her.

"And staring at your coffee helps with that?"

She lifted her chin and looked directly at him. "Anything else I'm doing wrong that you want to comment on?"

"What? No." He frowned. "I was just teasing. I'm sorry."

Of course he'd been teasing. What was *wrong* with her? Why did he do this to her? She couldn't catch her balance.

"I'm sorry. I guess I just didn't have enough sleep last night." Another lame excuse. She wasn't entirely pleased with his effect on her. Not at all.

SHE WAS A TESTY LITTLE THING. He'd better be careful what he said around her. Not that he'd be around her very often. He'd already decided that much. For some reason, she got under his skin, and he did not need that. Not now.

He'd already realized that he'd offended her —and probably Nora—when he'd blurted out that she should ask about money before accepting a job. He couldn't help it. It was like his mind was constantly in business mode, juggling numbers and time. But of course, Nora would pay her fairly. He was an idiot. He should keep his comments to himself.

"So, I hear the roof is going to be put on the building this week." Nora interrupted his thoughts.

"Yes, ma'am." If he could just get his supplier to deliver the materials.

"That's great. Then you can get started on the inside, too, right?"

"That's the plan." He reached for his coffee and bumped into Cece's hand. She snatched it away like he'd burned her. He grabbed his mug and took a gulp of the steaming coffee. He choked.

Darn, that was hot. He gingerly put the mug back on the table, careful not to touch Cece again.

He glanced at her and noticed she was trying her best to smother a grin. Great. She'd probably thought he was going to spit the hot coffee out all over the table.

"It's really good coffee here at the lodge, isn't it?" Her innocent tone didn't fool him.

"Darn tasty," he muttered.

"You should try the biscuits and gravy," Nora urged him. "I haven't figured out a way to deliver that all hot to you over at the building site."

"That sounds good. I'll have that."

"And some eggs?" Nora asked.

The woman did love to feed him. "Okay, yes, I'll have some eggs with it, too."

Nora's smile said her job was done. "Perfect."

"I think I'll have the biscuits and gravy, too." Cece placed her order with the waitress.

He would have thought she was an egg white, whole wheat toast, and a couple of pieces of fruit eater. She was just a slip of a woman. Though, she had mentioned she loved Nora's pies.

"You're staring at me." Cece eyed him.

"What? No, I'm not."

"You were."

"Nope, just thinking. Not looking at anything." Especially not looking at her warm brown eyes, or the way that one wayward lock of hair had escaped her braid thingie today and tenderly curled at the side of her face. Especially not any of that. And he especially didn't want to reach over and tuck that wayward lock back into her braid.

The entire breakfast of the delicious biscuits and gravy he especially didn't look at Cece. Not even when she wiped some crumbs from her face with a delicate swipe of her hand or when she laughed at something Bree said and it accentuated her dimple. Not even then.

He rose as soon as he swallowed the last bite,

almost knocking his chair over in his haste. "I better get going. Got lots to do. Nora, thanks for the breakfast."

He fled the dining hall... much like the way Cece had scurried away yesterday...

CHAPTER 4

C ece stood in her Denver apartment the next afternoon stunned into inertia. She'd marched into her boss's office this morning and turned in her notice. Even told him she could stay six weeks if that would help with filling her position. Her boss had come by her desk an hour later and told her to pack her things. They were letting her go today. Didn't want her to stay and work her last four weeks.

Maybe they thought she would steal clients, but what she'd need with them in Sweet River Falls was beyond her.

But now the four weeks she had to process all the change and deal with the actual move to Sweet River Falls... well, there was nothing keeping her here in Denver any longer.

She still stood just looking around the apartment. That wasn't helping anything. She should make a plan. A list of everything she needed to do. She should move from this spot. She really should. Find her notebook. Still, she stood as if her feet wouldn't listen to her.

The timing was actually great. She'd been dating Eric Riley off and on for a year or so and he wanted more than she was willing to give. Her heart wasn't into him. She'd slowly pulled away from him as she spent more weekends in Sweet River Falls. She'd actually told him last week that they should just be friends. He took it pretty well. At least she thought he had.

Anyway, she wanted to move to Sweet River Falls, she did. But the world seemed to be rushing at her. Her feet finally listened to her, and she crossed to the kitchen, pulled open a drawer, and grabbed a notebook and pen.

After fifteen minutes of planning, she felt a bit more under control. A tiny bit.

With a quick moment of decision, she went into her bedroom, packed up clothes, toiletries, and a couple of framed photos of Petey—*Pete*—was she ever going to get used to calling him that? She threw everything into some suitcases and boxes.

She needed to go to the cabin. Gain her equilibrium. Then she could deal with the details. She'd planned to be back in Sweet River Falls this coming weekend anyway to help her sister. This would give her more time and they could work on the business. Make plans. Get organized.

Feeling more in control, she carted her things to the car and headed off to the cabin in time to miss most of the rush hour traffic.

Her mind careened through thoughts and details on the drive, and before she knew it she was pulling into the drive at the cabin. Her sister was sitting on the swing by the lake and jumped up and crossed over to the car. "What are you doing here?"

"Well, it seems like I wasn't as irreplaceable at my job as I thought. I even offered to give them six weeks to find someone new. They walked me out of the office late this morning. Said I was finished." Cece stretched, tired from the drive, or the turmoil, or both.

"I see you loaded up." Bree eyed the full car.

"I did. I figured there was no reason to make a wasted trip. I've got clothes and some photos. Things I knew I wanted to keep."

"Let me help you get everything inside, then

we're going to sit out by the lake and watch the sunset, and you are going to relax."

"That sounds like a fabulous plan to me." She rubbed her shoulder, trying to erase the tension of the day.

Within half an hour she had changed into jeans and a sweater and they were sitting on the swing, sipping on Pinot Grigio.

"Did you get a chance to tell Eric about the move? You okay with moving away from him? I know you've been dating him for a while."

"I talked to him last week. Before I even knew I was moving. Told him we should just be friends. I just don't feel about him the way I know he wants me to feel."

"Then it's probably best you broke things off. You still think you can be friends?"

"I honestly don't know. I'm not sure he'd be someone who I'd really be friends with. Which was part of the problem with dating him. If we weren't friends, too, you know?"

"I do. Jason and I were friends first."

"And now, look at you two."

"Look at us." Bree smiled.

"You think we can really make this work? Make enough to support both of us?" Cece lazily pushed the swing with her foot, excitement of starting this new life, mixed in with exhaustion of the day and the feeling of not having everything under control.

"Would it make you feel better if I said I got three more catering gigs for next month? Oh, and a mid-week wedding at Pine View B&B next week. A last-minute elopement with only ten people. I was going to call you and say that I told the bride you'd call her tomorrow night to firm up the details. But here you are. I don't even have to call you." Bree smiled.

"That does make me feel better."

"It's going to work out. You'll see. I already have more business than I can handle alone."

Cece relaxed and let the peace of the evening wrap around her like her grandmother's favorite quilt. It all was going to work out.

It was.

Probably.

CHAPTER 5

Cece and Bree sat at the kitchen table finishing up their coffee. Cece smothered a yawn. The stress of yesterday hadn't quite been erased with her restless night's sleep.

"You look tired." Bree looked at her.

"A bit. I'll perk up soon." She looked at the old clock on the wall, a gift to her mother from her father. So many memories within these walls. She was going to have to get used to actually living here, instead of just trips here to visit family. "We should probably get going."

"We should." Bree stood but then reached for her cell phone when it rang. "Hello?" A smile spread across her face. "Hey, Madeline. Wow, it's great to hear from you."

Madeline, their cousin. Cece hadn't talked

to her since Madeline and her fiancé, Gil, had come to visit this past winter.

"You want to get married here? That's wonderful!" Bree's eyes lit up. "We have the perfect venue for you. They're putting up a new building at the lodge—*a chalet.*" Bree winked at her. "It's going to be great."

Cece watched as a frown then crossed Bree's face as she listened to Madeline.

"I could see if we can make that happen. I'm not quite sure if the chalet will be all finished by then. That's a week or so before we have our first wedding scheduled there."

Bree paced as she listened to Madeline. "Okay, let me see what I can do. Are you okay with having it outside or maybe in the main room of the lodge if the venue isn't finished?"

Cece watched as Bree listened and paced some more.

"Okay, let me see what I can do. I'll talk to Nora at the lodge and call you back. Oh, and hey, lucky for you, Cece is doing the wedding planning for the lodge so she can help you out. She's actually moved back here to Sweet River Falls."

Bree smiled. "Okay, I'll tell her. Talk to you soon."

Bree turned to her. "Maddy says hi, and good decision to move here. You know how she loves this area. Remember when she and her parents would come to visit us at the cabin when we were younger?"

"Yep, those were good times." Cece rose and grabbed her coffee cup. "So she wants to get married here?"

"Yes, this summer. I'm going to talk to Nora and see if we can squeeze them in. Madeline said it won't be too large. Family and some friends. So if the building isn't finished, they're happy to have it outside or in the great room at the lodge."

"Let's head over and talk to Nora." Cece set her cup in the sink. "Want to walk? It's a beautiful morning."

"Let's."

The girls walked out into the sunshine and up the ridge between their cabin and the lodge. They paused at the top and looked out over the lake. "It's so peaceful up here." Cece sighed.

"It is. I just love this place and everything about it. The town, the lake…"

"And Jason." Cece grinned.

"That, too."

They headed down the far side of the ridge

and entered the lodge. Nora looked up from the reception desk as they entered the lodge. "Good morning." Nora motioned them over. "Cece, what are you doing here on a Tuesday morning?"

"Let's just say that my company didn't take my turning in my notice very well. They let me go." Cece shrugged.

"Their loss, our gain." Nora paused and cocked her head to one side.

"So, since you're here. I was wondering... could I hire you to order the furniture and fixtures for the new building? I have a guy ordering the tech stuff like the sound system, but I need help with the rest. I loved what you did to sparkle up our outside setup for weddings. You think you could work your magic on our inside setup? Something simple but tasteful and stylish for the weddings?"

"I'd love to." This was great. She'd feel like she was pulling her weight with the business. Bringing in new money, not just helping Bree out.

"We have other news," Bree added.

"What's that?"

"Our cousin Madeline called. Do you

remember her and her fiancé, Gil? They were here this winter and stayed at the lodge."

"I do. Lovely girl."

"Well, they want to get married here. This summer. I think Gil finally insisted they should really pick a date. I said I'd look into seeing if we could squeeze them in as our first wedding in the chalet.

Nora grinned. "So the Chalet at the Lodge is really growing on you."

Bree nodded. "I do like it."

"I do too. I think you have officially named it." Nora looked thoughtful. "We should get Jason to add the official name to the website."

"And it would be so nice if the first one was Maddy's."

"That's fine with me. Did you check the online schedule?"

"I did. You're free the weekend before our first scheduled wedding at the new building."

"Well, we'd have to check with Zach. He hasn't said anything about being behind schedule. And we padded the first wedding by a couple of weeks after he said he'd be finished. But, Cece, you'd have to really get started on ordering for the inside."

"I can do that. It would be so wonderful for Maddy to have her wedding there."

"Why don't you go and look over the building? You can talk to Zach. He'll tell you where he's planned the wiring for lights and whatever else you need. And Jason will hook you up with some of our suppliers and you can price out what we'll need." Nora paused and turned to greet some guests who walked up to the desk. She turned back to Cece. "Can you ask Zach if he can manage to have it ready the week before we had planned?"

Great, let her be the bearer of that news. "Sure thing." She turned to Bree. "I guess we're really doing this." Cece grinned.

Bree smiled. "I guess we are. I'll call Madeline. And see how many rooms she'll want reserved here at the lodge, too. Or if the lodge doesn't have enough room, there's Pine View B&B."

Cece nodded and headed out of the lodge. She stopped in her tracks when she realized the one tiny flaw in her newly acquired project.

She'd have to work with Zach.

And she wasn't sure if that was a good thing or a bad thing.

ZACH HAD a full crew in today, putting on the roof to the new building. At least that part was going right. Now if the picture windows he'd ordered would come in, that would make him mighty pleased. But for some reason, his order had been canceled—and not by him. He'd talked to the supplier who swore they had no idea how it happened and he must have canceled the order himself.

Only he hadn't. They'd worked with him to put a rush order on the new windows, but he'd be cutting it close.

"Hi."

He twirled around at the sound of her voice. He'd recognized it instantly. And that kind of bugged him. "Hi. What are you doing here?"

"That seems to be a popular question. I turned in my notice and they thought it best that I leave… so here I am."

He frowned. "They just let you go?"

"They did. Guess I wasn't as valuable as I thought I was."

He could see a tiny smidge of hurt in her eyes. Well her former employer was a fool.

Anyone could tell she was a hard worker and a good person.

Though… he didn't really know that, did he? He didn't even know her. Not really. Except the soft tones of her voice and the sweet melody of her laugh had stayed with him since he'd scurried away on Sunday. Scurried. That word again. He shook his thoughts away.

"Well, that's too bad about your job, but since you're going to start working with your sister, it's not all bad, is it?"

"No, not bad. I was just a bit shocked. I'm getting over it though." Cece swiveled around slowly, taking in the building. "I see part of the roof is up."

"We're working on it. Hope to have it under roof soon." He glanced up to where he could still see the bright blue Colorado sky through the opening above him. With any luck it would be finished before the big spring storm they were predicting at the end of the week. Sheeting up today and shingles started tomorrow… if the shingle delivery actually came today like it was supposed to. He glanced at his watch. "Was there something you needed? I need to get back to work."

"Oh, and Nora wanted me to tell you that

we've booked another wedding here a week before the first one we had scheduled. It's my cousin's wedding. She said you hadn't said anything about delays and that she was sure you could have it ready by then because we'd planned a two-week buffer in for you to finish."

He gritted his teeth. He was already stressed about getting it ready in time. Now they'd upped his deadline. He glanced at his watch again. "Any other surprises?"

WELL, that wasn't very subtle. He'd let her know she was taking up his valuable time. But he did have a surprise coming. "Yes, I actually came to see you—*at Nora's request.*" She paused to let the words sink in.

He quit looking at his stupid watch and paused. "What does Nora need?"

"She's hired me to fix the inside of the building. Pick out the fixtures. And I'll be ordering the furniture for weddings and meetings. Chairs, tables. We'll need some kind of arbor or something built—I'm thinking removable—that we can put in front of those big picture windows." She looked out the large gaping hole. "Or... where the windows will be."

"You?" He eyed her.

"Yes, I'm actually quite good at pulling things together decorating-wise. And Nora doesn't have time to do it herself. I appreciate her giving me a chance on this. I'm not going to disappoint her." Cece stood tall—well, as tall as her five foot three inches would allow. "She wants me to coordinate that with you. Well, not the furniture, but the fixtures."

"I see." He did not look pleased. Not one bit.

"So do you have time to go over where we'll need fixtures? I'd like to do some looking around and find just the perfect ones for high up in these rafters."

"And you think you can get them ordered and brought here in time?" He looked at her. "We were just going to put in some track lighting along the rafters."

"Well, show me, and we'll talk about it."

"I—" He glanced at his darn watch again. "Fine, I'll give a brief tour so you can see what's planned and take it from there."

She took out her notebook and started taking notes as he walked her around. It was clear he was proud of his handiwork. Every doorjamb was square, the window openings plumb. Everything was finished perfectly. It was obvious he was a stickler for details. Her father had given her an appreciation of fine construction and woodworking, and it was clear that Zach's work was top-notch.

He loosened up a bit as he led her around. He even quit looking at his watch every five seconds as he proudly showed off the details of the chalet.

"I really love this building. It's going to be a great addition to the lodge. You're doing a really good job on it."

She almost laughed when his chest puffed out like when she complimented a young boy.

"Thanks. I do like doing the job right."

"That's the only way to do it, isn't it?" They at least agreed on something. "I think I have enough notes now. I'm going to head back to the lodge and see if I can catch Jason."

"Let me know if you need anything else." He nodded and turned away before she even could thank him.

Okay then. Back to business. The man was all business, all the time.

CHAPTER 6

Z ach fumed the rest of the afternoon and evening. It was getting dark, and he'd have to quit. He knew part of it was his own fault. He'd never let on about the delays. Jason and Nora had taken a chance on him with this project. His first solo project without his partner. He had no plans on disappointing them. He'd hire more workers or drive a darn truck into Denver himself to get the building materials. He'd finish it on time.

Well, now he'd finish it one week early…

He packed up his tools all the while ineffectively wishing for another couple hours of daylight.

"Hey, Zach."

He turned to see Jason standing under the

half-finished roofed part of the building. Not finished roof, mind you, because another worker had gone home sick. "Hey, Jason. What's up?"

"Just checking on the progress. Mom said we booked in another wedding a week earlier than planned. You good with that?"

"I'm good with that." No, he wasn't. What he wanted was an extra month or so to finish the project, not one less week. But he wouldn't say that.

"Great. I'm glad the project is going so smoothly."

Yep, smooth as a raw, split, splintery log...

"You finished up?"

"For today."

"Come on, I'll walk you back to the lodge. I saw your truck parked there."

That's right. He'd left it there after consuming a huge breakfast at the dining hall. The last meal he'd had today. His stomach growled as if to chastise him.

"Sure, let's go."

They walked along the path by the lake, a cool breeze rippling the top of the water. Jason paused on the pathway. "I swear, this view never gets old. There really is going to be a great view from the new building."

"Can't argue with you there." He paused beside Jason, admiring the lake and the beginning of the stars, twinkling above them in the sky.

"I really appreciate what a good job you're doing, Zach."

Great, no pressure. "Thanks."

They continued over to the main building at the lodge and Nora came down the steps with Cece. He wasn't amused at his immediate reaction to seeing Cece again. His pulse started to race. Which was *not* what it was supposed to do.

"Hi, Zach." Nora welcomed him.

"Hey, Nora, Cece."

"You know, it's getting late. Why don't you and Cece have dinner here at the lodge? You can talk business. My treat."

"Oh, I should probably—" Cece stopped in her tracks.

"No, I need—" He searched for an excuse.

"Nonsense. You both have to eat. Come on inside. Jason, you joining them?"

"I'm headed over to see Bree."

"Okay, it's just Cece and Zach, then." Nora led the way into the dining hall and Zach trudged behind.

49

He loved Nora's meals. There was nothing unusual about having a meal at the lodge.

Why did he feel like he was walking into an ambush of his own making?

AN AWKWARD SILENCE fell over them after they ordered. Cece stared at her iced tea and concentrated on the melodious tinkling of the ice against the side of the glass when she stirred the drink. Not that it needed stirring. She hadn't added any sugar to it.

The man made her jumpy, off-center, unsure of herself. And she hated that feeling. She needed to be in control. If only she could put him on one of her ever-present to-do lists and sort him out like she sorted out her tasks.

She shook her head. That didn't even make any sense. He rattled her thoughts, too. She squeezed lemon into her tea with a bit more vigor than she intended, and it squirted on her shirt as the tangy, citrusy aroma surrounded her.

"Why are you glaring at me?"

"What?" She looked up at him.

"Glaring. You keep glaring at me."

"No, I'm not."

"You are. Even more than you're glaring at your wayward lemon slice."

She sighed. "Well, maybe…"

"What did I do?" He cocked his head to one side.

"You—" Did she dare say her thoughts out loud? "I can't figure you out."

"What's to figure out? I'm a simple man."

As if. "No, you're actually not. You go from being all friendly and helpful to acting like I'm a bother. The look on your face when Nora suggested we had dinner together… let's just say it wasn't the most excited I've ever seen a man get about having a meal with me."

He pushed back his chair and stretched out his long legs. One of them bumped against hers. She kept herself from jerking away while she watched the emotions slip across his face. Embarrassment, thoughtfulness, then a look of what? Resignation? That wasn't much better than his I-don't-want-to-eat-with-her look.

He let out a long breath. "I'm sorry. It's just… you throw me off balance."

Well, that was more honest than she'd expected. And strangely, it made her feel more in control if he felt off-balance around her, too.

He looked at her closely, as if trying to decide if he should continue. She could tell the moment he decided with an almost imperceptible nod. "The project—the building for Jason and Nora—it's a big project. The first one I've had on my own. I've always had a business partner. I'm trying my best to keep on schedule and... let's just say I've had a few curveballs to deal with."

"Where is your partner now?"

"He—he moved away."

"You two had a falling out?"

"You could say that. He moved away... with... uh, my girlfriend."

Ouch. That had to hurt. "I'm sorry." Though, she really had no clue. No one had ever cheated on her. She'd actually done the cheating... but that was behind her. Way behind her. She'd moved on and forgiven herself. Mostly.

"It wasn't the best time of my life. But better it happened when it did." Much better. Because he'd actually been thinking of asking his girlfriend to marry him. Which was ridiculous, because as he found out, she'd been cheating on him for months. What did he know about women and honesty?

And why was he even telling Cece this?

"So, this is your first project without a partner?"

"Yes. Jason was good to give me the chance. Berry and Saunders Construction became Berry Construction. And I hear that Saunders Construction opened up in Boulder." Hopefully far enough away to not be any competition and, even more important, far enough away that he'd see neither Saunders nor his ex.

"Had you dated her very long?"

"Two years. But whatever. I never really knew her it seems. Anyway, it was a year ago. My partner and I had to wrap up some projects we had going at the time, then he left." He changed the subject. "How about you? Anyone special in your life?"

"No. All free and clear to move here to Sweet River Falls."

And he wasn't sure that he liked the tiny trill of excitement that flitted through him when she said she didn't have a boyfriend. Because that was silly. He'd sworn off women. But this woman sitting across the table from him, with her one dimple and dancing eyes made him think that maybe, just maybe, his decision to swear off women forever was just a bit too hasty.

She smiled at him then and he wavered under her magic spell. "So what else do I need to know about Zach Berry?"

Okay, he could talk about himself. Anything to keep from getting lost in her eyes. "I was born and raised in Denver. Came here about ten years ago. Started working construction, then opened up our own company with my partner."

"Family?"

"My parents retired to Florida. I have a sister still in Denver. You have any other siblings besides Bree? Parents around here?"

A sadness drifted across her face. "I have a sister, Abby, in Los Angeles. But my parents are gone. Killed in a car crash a little over a year ago."

"I'm sorry. Both at once? That must have been hard."

"It was. It *is*." Tears glistened in her eyes and she looked down at her drink. "Anyway, I guess it just takes time."

Before he could say more, the waitress arrived with their food. But really, what more could he say than he was sorry? He couldn't imagine it. He still made at least a yearly trek to Florida to see his parents. Usually in the winter when the construction business slowed down and the sunny Florida weather beckoned him. But he hadn't made time this winter. He'd been too busy. He vowed right then to make plans to go see his folks as soon as the building at the lodge was finished.

Cece was concentrating on eating her meal and the hint of tears in her eyes disappeared. He attacked the fried chicken on his plate and turned to mindless talk of the weather and the upcoming May Festival. Much safer topics.

He watched her smile at the stories he told about past May Festivals and started listing off all the events the town had each year.

"There's a lot more than I remember from when I was here as a young girl. You almost need a calendar to keep track of the numerous festivals and fair weekends and special events now."

"Yep, there's a calendar out on the town's website."

She grabbed her bag hanging on the back

of her chair and scribbled a note on the pad she took out. She looked up at him. "Just making a note to check out the website. I figure it will be good to know what's going on in the town and what are super busy weekends."

Of course she was writing a note. That seemed to be her thing. He'd seen her writing lots of notes when he'd shown her around the building at the lodge. He liked organized people.

They finished their dinner, and he walked her out to her car.

"That was nice. I mean, I enjoyed having dinner with you." She stood next to her car with the door open but didn't slip inside.

"It was nice. Much better than grabbing something at home. I admit to eating standing up at the sink quite often when I get home late."

"No, you don't." She looked horrified.

"Okay, then maybe I didn't admit that." He smiled.

"No wonder Nora tries to feed you all the time."

"I'm sure not complaining about that."

She slipped into her car and looked up at him. "Well, I guess I'll see you tomorrow."

"Yes."

She pulled the door shut and drove away. He stood there in the moonlight like a fool. *Yes?* That's the only thing he could think to say to her?

What he'd really wanted to do was to ask her to stay longer. Maybe go for a walk. Or even ask her out on a date.

But that was ridiculous because he'd sworn off women, right?

The heck with that stupid swearing off women thing. He *liked* this woman. He wanted to see more of her. Maybe he *would* ask her out.

He whistled as he headed over to his truck, for once not concentrating on all the delays at the project.

Cece entered the cabin, lost in thought.

"Hey, there you are. Did Nora feed you again? If not, there's some chicken in the fridge." Bree looked up from the table. "You okay?"

"What? Yes, I'm fine." She focused on Bree's words and not Zach's tantalizing smile and warm eyes that lit up when he talked about his business.

"And yet, your face says something is going on."

"I thought you were going out with Jason tonight." She avoided her sister's question.

"He came over for a while. But he was exhausted, so I sent him home."

"You should set a wedding date so that when he comes home at night, he stays." She grabbed a wine glass from the cabinet and walked over to sit at the table by her sister. Bree slid the wine bottle over to her.

"That's what Jason said. I've just been so busy, and there are so many details in planning a wedding. I can't imagine adding that to my already crazy schedule." Bree shook her head.

"And yet, you have your own personal wedding planner sitting right here at the table with you." Cece poured some wine and took a sip. "Oh, that's good."

"A new wine I wanted to try out. I'm always getting asked suggestions on wines to go with my catered offerings."

"Well, this one is a winner. Maybe we can serve it at your wedding." Cece grinned.

Bree let out a sigh. "I'll figure it out soon. I do want to marry Jason. I—and this sounds terrible—I want to *be* married to Jason more than have the wedding."

"Is this because it's your second marriage?"

"No, it's just… I don't know. I'm pretty overwhelmed with life right now."

"I'm here to help. Take things over where I can."

"And I'm very grateful." Bree set her glass down. "But you're still avoiding my question.

"What question?"

"What's up?"

Cece laughed. "Well, I did have dinner at the lodge. With Zach."

"And?" Bree cocked an eyebrow.

"And… well… we talked. He's an interesting guy. Nice."

"I thought you said he was all business and cold."

"Maybe I changed my mind."

A smile teased the corner of Bree's mouth. "Maybe you have. You going to see him again? Go out with him?"

"I'm sure I'll see him tomorrow at the lodge. But I just met him. It's not like we're dating or anything."

"But you like him."

"I don't *dislike* him." Cece stuck to her story, unwilling to admit Zach intrigued her. The first guy she'd really been interested in—in forever it seemed. And that included Eric Riley, because though she'd gone out with him and it had been fun to have someone to go out to the movies with or go out and grab a bite to eat with… she'd never really been interested in him. Not like that.

Bree rose. "I'm going to bed. *Sweet dreams,*" she said pointedly.

"Subtle, Bree. Very subtle."

CHAPTER 7

N ora looked up from the reception desk to see her friend Annie standing in front of her. "Annie, hi. I wasn't expecting you."

"You've been so busy you haven't stopped by Bookish Cafe in weeks. I miss you. I figured if I showed up and demanded coffee, that maybe you'd take a break."

She looked at the stack of paperwork she'd been sorting through. She'd been busy and had been neglecting her friend who was undoubtedly just as busy as she was.

Jason walked up to them. "Hey, Annie. Good to see you."

"I've come to steal your mother. Just for a bit. Maybe a cup of coffee's worth of time."

"Great. Mom, I'll cover the desk. You go

have coffee with Annie. You two should take it outside, it's a beautiful day out there. Sunshine and warming up nicely."

"Okay, thanks. I'll be back in soon."

"Take your time. I got this." Jason walked behind the reception desk.

Nora grabbed them both some coffee and they headed outside into the sunshine. "Want to go sit by the lake?"

"Sounds great."

They wandered down the path to the lake and settled on one of the wooden benches along the shoreline. She took a sip of the coffee, relishing taking a few minutes away from work.

"I love this view," Annie sighed as they both sat and looked out over the lake.

"Me, too. So peaceful."

"Any more news about the zoning changes to the lake?"

Nora shook her head. "No news so far, but I know that Dobbs is pressing on with it."

"Well, we'll have to do all we can to cut him off."

"I've been talking to some business owners in town. Some of them are for the zoning changes. They think it will bring more business to town. You know, the ones who don't actually live on the lake or have businesses on the lake. They don't appreciate how wonderful the peacefulness of the lake is."

"I'll never understand how people want to build up and expand and destroy the quiet and natural beauty of an area."

"Progress." Nora shrugged. "Anyway, how's Nick?"

"He's out of town at a convention. It's strange. I was so used to being alone. So many years of it... Now that Nick and I are married... well, it seems strange to rattle around in the house at night all by myself. I'll be glad when he comes home tomorrow."

"You should come to dinner tonight. Beth, Mac, and the boys are coming over. I'm cooking. Say you'll come."

Annie grinned. "I'll come."

"Great. We're eating about six."

"I'll be there." Annie sipped her coffee. "How's the new building coming along?"

"Fine. I can't wait for it to be finished. Zach is doing a great job on it."

"I think it was such a great idea and a good addition to the lodge."

"Did you hear Cece Stuart is moving to town?"

"No, really?"

"She's going to join Bree in her business."

"I'm glad to see the sisters have worked things out."

"Cece's such a great girl. I keep thinking of reasons to have her work with Zach."

Annie laughed. "Always the matchmaker."

"I think they're a good fit for each other. I just have this hunch about them. And it never hurts to give people a little push."

Nora turned and looked at the lake again. The sunshine threw sparkles of light dancing across the water. The light breeze tickled the branches of the trees along the water's edge. She hoped with every fiber of her being that she could keep the lake like it was right this very minute. Peaceful. Beautiful. No noisy motorboats or jet skis. No high-rise condo buildings.

There were times when she believed Sweet River Falls needed progress and to change with the times, but ruining this lake wasn't one of them.

Annie stood. "I should let you get back to work, and I need to get back to the bookstore."

They walked back up to the lodge and Nora gave her friend a quick hug. "Thanks for coming by and dragging me away from my work." She watched Annie drive away then headed back inside to tackle the stack of paperwork.

CECE HEADED over to the new building carrying a large picnic basket filled with lunch for Zach. She was beginning to think Nora thought she was a delivery person. Though she had to admit she liked having the excuse to see Zach again. She climbed up on the long porch that stretched across the opening to the chalet and stepped inside. She looked up and only saw one small portion of sky still visible.

"Zach?" She called out over the sound of hammering on the roof. That probably wasn't going to work. She headed across the building to look in the kitchen area at the far end.

She peeked in and saw Zach perched on a stool by a table made out of sawhorses and a sheet of plywood, poring over a large rolled out paper. "Zach?"

He looked up and flipped her a quick smile. "Hey."

This time his voice was warm and

welcoming, and he hadn't looked at his watch… yet…

"Nora wanted me to bring you lunch."

He laughed his warm chuckle of a laugh. "Gotta love that woman." He rolled up the papers in front of him and she set the basket on the table.

He looked in the basket and started unloading the food. "She sent enough for an army."

"I might have mentioned you standing up at your kitchen sink to eat…" She grinned at him.

He unwrapped the sandwiches. "Want to join me?"

She did want to sit with him—spend some time with him—but she'd had a late breakfast and really wasn't hungry. But then, the sandwiches did look good. "I… maybe a little bit."

He grabbed another stool, placed it by the makeshift table, and she joined him.

"How are your plans coming along?"

"Pretty good. I've already ordered the chairs. Bree gave me a list of what's needed for the kitchen. I'm still undecided on the light fixtures. And I'm not sure on the tables but don't have much time to make up my mind. I'm thinking round might be better for weddings—for the receptions—but maybe not for meetings. Trying to sort all that out."

"You've really gotten a lot done in a short time."

"Lists. The secret of my success."

He laughed and grabbed a yellow pad of paper sitting on the table. "I'm a list maker myself. Used to try and juggle it all in my head, and most of it is still up there, but this way I don't forget anything."

A young, tired-looking worker poked his head into the kitchen area. "Hey, boss. Shingles are here."

"Have them unload them out front, thanks." Zach stood and grabbed his sandwich. "That was Billy. He's got a newborn. Looks like it, too, doesn't he?"

"He does have that new-father exhausted look."

"I told him he should take another week of leave with pay but he wouldn't hear of it. He knew we're busy with this job. Anyway, I guess I'm going to have to eat and run. I need to check this order, sorry about that."

"No problem. I'm going to just take a few

more measurements, then I'll be out of your way."

"You're not in my way," he assured her and turned and walked out of the opening that would soon be the door.

Well, things were improving. Instead of being annoyed she was interrupting him, he'd admitted she wasn't in his way.

She finished the few bites of sandwich and went out to recount the number of windows— or would-be windows—and measure the floor space again to plan out how many chairs could be set out in how many rows and how wide the aisle would be. No use trying to figure that out at Madeline's wedding.

Nora had loved the lanterns she'd gotten for outside weddings, so she was going to look into some battery run lanterns for along the aisle for evening weddings. She also still needed to talk to Zach about the arbor. She wanted to string fairy lights through it and the brides could pick what kind of flowers to put on it.

She headed back to the kitchen area to find Zach. She paused when she heard him talking on his phone.

"No, they are not the right shingles. I know they're a close shade, but not the ones I ordered.

And they aren't the same quality, either. I'm not interested in a break in price to keep these. I want what I ordered, and I need them like yesterday." He clicked off his phone and tossed it on a pile of papers on the table.

She walked into the room. "Everything okay?"

He looked up, annoyance hovering in his eyes. "Yes." He raked his fingers through his hair. "Well, no. They delivered the wrong shingles. Roofing is not where we want to cut corners on this building. Not with the harsh winters. The supplier is looking into when he can get the right shingles here." He raked his hand through his hair. "Another delay."

"Another one?"

A guilty look flashed across his face.

"Are you having problems?"

"Nothing I can't handle. Don't worry about it."

She frowned. "Okay, but I thought everything was going well and there was no problem adding on Madeline's wedding." Her mind started racing ahead to what they'd have to do if the building wasn't finished in time for the weddings that had been booked at the chalet.

"I'll have it finished in time."

She'd never seen a more determined look on anyone's face, so she chose to believe him.

"I guess I'll leave you to get back to work." She turned to leave.

"Was there something you needed?"

"It can wait." She wasn't about to pile anything else on him right now. Discussion of the arbor could wait.

He was already engrossed in the papers scattered on the table in front of him before she even got to the doorway.

ZACH TOSSED his pencil on the makeshift table. He needed to move crew around. He'd had a full schedule for tomorrow to put on the shingles. Now that wasn't going to happen. The windows were days if not a full week from being delivered, as well as the doors. If the storm they were predicting came in, he'd have to secure all the openings with plastic. Just another thing to add to the list.

He sat up and stretched, sure this job was trying to kill him. At the sound of a crash and a scream, he bounded up, sending the stool reeling across the floor. He ran out into the main area of the building. His heart plummeted when he saw Cece sprawled out on the floor, and he raced to cover the distance and knelt beside her. "Cece? You okay?" Her eyes were closed.

She slowly opened them and focused on him. "Yes…" She didn't sound very certain.

He saw the ladder sprawled out beside her. "Were you climbing on the ladder?"

"Mm-hmm."

"Why?"

"Taking some measurements." She started to sit up.

"Wait. Are you sure you're okay?"

"Just my ego is bruised."

"You need to stay off my ladders."

"I'm sorry. I didn't want to bother you." She sat all the way up and looked at her hands, flexing her wrists. "See, nothing's broken."

"You're lucky you didn't get hurt worse, and you're not a bother to me." He didn't know why he added that. But she wasn't a bother. He liked having her around. Though he was positively going to forbid her to climb a ladder again. Not that she seemed like a woman who would take being forbidden to do anything with any kind of good grace. Maybe he'd just make it a strong *suggestion*.

"Well, if I'm not a bother, how about helping me up off the floor?"

He jumped up and gently helped her to her feet, watching her closely for any sign of injury. "You sure you're okay?"

"I'm fine." She reached down and picked up her notebook. "I'll let you get back to work."

But he didn't want to leave her. His heart was still hammering from the sight of her just lying on the floor.

"Anyway, thanks for the rescue. I'm going to head back to the lodge and talk to Nora about some ideas I had." She started to walk away.

"Cece, wait."

She paused and turned back toward him.

"I was wondering… if you… if you might want to get something to eat. You know, like go out to dinner. Like not here at the lodge. Go out. A date." He stammered like a teenager asking a girl out for the first time.

"Sure. When?"

"Tonight?" That was too soon, wasn't it? Women needed advance notice. Did he sound too eager? Heck, he was a mess.

"Tonight sounds great."

His eyes widened. "It does?"

Amused laughter escaped her lips. "Yes, it does."

"I could pick you up about six?"

"Six would work. Do you know where I live?"

"Jason said it's around the bend on the cove?"

"It is. We have a red mailbox. A sign says Stuart Chateau. But don't worry. It's a grandiose name for a nice simple cabin. My mom named it. She loved it so much…" A sad smile crossed her lips. "Anyway, I'll see you tonight."

"Yes."

She turned and walked away.

Yes? Was that the only answer he was able to give to this woman?

CHAPTER 8

Cece regretted her choice of clothes she'd brought with her to the cabin. Work clothes. A pair of cowboy boots that were broken in and oh so comfortable. Simple black pants to wear when she helped Bree with her catering events. But nothing date-worthy. She stared into the closet as if her fairy godmother would wave a wand and suddenly the perfect outfit would appear.

Bree walked into the bedroom. "What's up? You're just staring into that closet."

"I'm…" She turned to face her sister. "I'm kinda going on a date tonight."

Bree grinned. "With Zach, right?"

"Right."

"So what's the problem?"

"I have nothing to wear. Nothing. I didn't bring anything even remotely appropriate for a date."

"Never fear, little sister. I've got this. Follow me."

Cece did as she was told and followed her sister into her bedroom. Bree threw open her closet and tugged out a sweater in a lovely shade of light peach. "This will work. And I have a printed scarf that goes with it."

"But what pants? Yours won't fit me. I'm so much shorter than you. And I don't even have nice shoes to wear." She almost moaned but took the offered clothes.

"Wear your cowboy boots. And your dark skinny jeans. You're in Sweet River Falls. We're not a get all dressed up for dates kind of town."

Cece went back to her room and slipped on her outfit. Bree was right. It was the perfect combination of nice, but not too dressy. She turned this way and that looking at herself in the mirror. She couldn't remember the last time she cared this much about what she wore or had been this excited for a date.

Bree poked her head in the doorway. "You ready?"

"I am. I think. Gosh, I'm so nervous. Do I look okay?"

"You look like your cute, adorable self."

Cece rolled her eyes.

"Come on. Let's get you out into the great room. There's more room for you to pace out there," Bree teased.

She froze when she heard the knock at the door. "He's early…"

Bree glanced at her watch. "Five minutes. And you're ready. So… what's the problem?"

"I'm… *not* ready." Her heart pounded, and she looked in the mirror yet again.

Bree walked into the room and hugged her. "Yes. Yes, you are. Now come on." She grabbed her hand and led her out of the room.

ZACH STOOD AT THE DOOR, shifting from foot to foot. He'd cleaned out his truck so that she wouldn't have to sit on a stack of tools or papers. He'd wanted to wash it, too, but had run out of time. He'd been lucky to get home, grab a shower, and get back here without being late.

He shuffled his feet again, running a hand down the side of his best jeans. He hadn't known what to wear, so settled on nice jeans—ones without holes worn in them like his work jeans—and a nice button-down shirt. He checked his reflection in the window beside the door and glanced at his watch.

The door popped open and Bree stood in the doorway. "Hey, Zach. Come on in."

He stepped into the cabin and glanced around in appreciation. It was homey and well designed. The entire back of the cabin was wall-to-wall windows and doors showing an expansive view of the lake. Someone had planned well on this cabin.

"Hi."

The sound of Cece's voice brought him out of his builder's evaluation of the cabin. She looked nice. *Really* nice. And she'd taken her hair out of that fancy braid thing and it drifted around her shoulders. He liked her hair down like that.

Had he even answered her? He'd been so lost in his thoughts. "Hi. You ready to go?"

"I am." She turned to Bree. "I won't be late. I know we have a lot to do tomorrow."

"Hey, I'm not your keeper. Stay out as late as you want." Bree walked them to the doorway. "Have fun."

He led Cece to his truck and helped her climb in. Not an easy feat with how high his truck rode off the ground. He hurried around and climbed into the driver's seat. "So, I thought we'd go to Antonio's?"

"Love Antonio's," Cece agreed.

An awkward silence stuffed its way into the cab of his pickup, smothering him. He could not think of a single thing to say to her. He was vividly aware that she was sitting just a foot or so away. A slight scent of some kind of flower wafted through the air, trying to break through the stifling silence.

They drove all the way into town without saying a word. This did not bode well for the evening.

WHAT WAS WRONG WITH HER? She could usually chat up anyone. But they pulled into a parking spot near Antonio's and hadn't said a word on the whole trip. Did he regret asking her out?

And he kept looking at his stupid watch.

He got out of the truck, came around, and opened her door. The smothering silence drifted out into the evening air and she drew a deep breath. He reached up a hand to help her, and she slipped her hand into his.

A flash of electricity jolted through her. She could see from his eyes he'd felt it too. She knew he had.

She slipped out of the truck, stepped onto the pavement, and bumped up against him. That did not help the lightning bolts racing through her veins.

She stepped back to put space between them, but the storm still swirled around her. He took her elbow as they started to walk down the sidewalk. She started to count her steps to ignore the heat of his hand on her arm.

One, two, three, four... where was she, again? One, two, three...

"You okay?"

She glanced up from her steps to look at him. "What? Yes."

"You seem to be concentrating on your steps."

"Oh, sorry. Uneven pavement." Which wasn't a total lie, it just wasn't what she was worried about...

He held the door open for her and she was almost—*almost*—glad for his hand to be off her arm. Almost.

Antonio greeted them as they stepped inside. "Welcome. Would you like a table in the back? Or you could wait for one by the window if you prefer."

"The back is fine," Zach answered, then turned to her. "That's okay with you?"

"Yes. That's fine." She rubbed her now lonely elbow.

They sat down, ordered margaritas, and browsed through the menu. She knew what she wanted, but she concentrated on the words on the page before her like she'd never eaten Mexican food before and needed to read every tiny detail about each and every item on the menu.

HE WATCHED her concentrate on the menu, her own hand resting on the table, mere inches away. He so wanted to reach out and touch it... but, no, that would be wrong. He'd just met her. This was their first date.

Still, he stared at her hand with a delicate almost nude shade of polish on her nails.

She glanced up from her menu and he averted his stare.

"I'm going to have some chicken tacos." She set down her menu.

"I think I'm going to have the steak fajitas."

"You think we could get a sopapilla for dessert?"

"With cinnamon, honey, and ice cream? I'm sure we could."

"Yes, exactly how I like it." She smiled, then looked down at the menu again.

The conversation lagged yet again. This was not how he planned it. He wanted them to have fun and relax and… you know, even talk…

"Did you get the shingle situation sorted out?"

Her question almost startled him. A conversation. Who knew? "I—I'm working on it. Hoping to have the right ones here next week, but the supplier can't guarantee it. If he can't come through, I'm canceling the order with him and getting them through someone else."

"Where did you learn to be a builder?"

"I started working in construction when I was still in high school. Worked for this great builder in Denver. Learned so much. Then when I decided to move up in the mountains, I found a job with a builder here in Sweet River

Falls, so I moved here. He retired and we started up Berry and Saunders."

"Do you like owning your own company?"

"I do. It's hard work though. It's like you never get away from it. I'm either working at the job site, or meeting with someone about a new job, or doing endless paperwork."

"I've always worked for someone else. This whole partnership with Bree is new. Honestly, I'm a little bit nervous about it. I hope it all works out."

He hoped it worked out for them, too. He knew personally how badly a partnership could go. But maybe it would be different since it was Cece's sister. "I'm sure it will work out. You both seem like hard workers. That's half the battle with owning a business. And being willing to accept you can never really step away from it."

She nodded. "I think that's why Bree is so overwhelmed now. She was trying to do so many things. Build the business, along with doing the actual baking and cooking for the catering, *and* trying to help brides plan their weddings."

"So you're taking over the wedding planning part?"

"That, and I help her with the cooking. I'm nowhere near the cook she is, but I can follow directions." Her warm brown eyes shone brightly in the flickering light of the candles on the table.

She looked beautiful in the candlelight. Heck, she looked beautiful in the sunlight. But what he really liked was the charismatic charm she had. It wove a spell around him, and he knew he was becoming helpless against it.

THEY WALKED out into the cool evening air after finishing their dinner. A shiver ran through her even though it wasn't really *that* chilly.

Zach placed his arm around her shoulder and tucked her up against him. "Let's get you to the truck and get you warmed up."

As far as she was concerned, she was fine right here where she was, tucked protectively up against his side. He slowed his stride to match hers and they headed for his truck which they reached all too quickly.

He opened the door, and she climbed inside. He gave her a smile as he closed her door. A smile that kept her warm until he climbed in beside her, turned on the motor, and flicked on the heat.

He drove her back to the cabin and that, too, they reached all too quickly. He turned off the motor, and they sat for a moment. She didn't want the evening to end.

She turned to face him on the seat. "Would you like to sit out by the lake for a bit? I can run in and grab a blanket. We have a swing my dad built down by the water's edge."

"I'd like that a lot." His deep voice rumbled over her.

She swallowed. "Okay, I'll be right back out." She jumped out of the truck and hurried into the house.

"You back so soon?" Bree looked up from the couch where she sat reading.

"I'm back, but we're going to sit out by the lake for a bit."

Bree leaned forward and Cece grabbed the quilt from the back of the couch. "I'll be in soon."

"Don't rush in on my account." Bree eyed her over her reading glasses, a smile teasing the corners of her mouth.

Cece hurried back outside, clutching the quilt close to her, her heart pounding in her chest. Why? All she was doing was going to sit by the lake with Zach. It was no big deal, right? And yet, it felt like a very big deal to her.

He stood in the moonlight by the truck, the light filtering down on him. She waited for her eyes to adjust to the dimness after the bright cabin lights, then crossed over to him. "Come on." She led him to the swing.

They settled on the swing and she dropped the quilt on their laps. He moved closer to her and reached across her to tuck the quilt against her legs. He set the swing into a gentle motion and she relaxed against the back of the swing. Or tried to. He draped his arm along the back of the swing, but she ignored it just inches away from her.

She shivered, but not from the cold.

He dropped his arm around her shoulder. "You cold?"

"No, I'm fine." She was fine. Perfectly, wonderfully fine. She hadn't been this fine in a long time.

"Looks like it's almost a full moon." His deep voice wrapped around her.

She glanced up. "It does."

"You've got a beautiful view here."

"It never disappoints." But it had never looked this wonderful, either.

She settled against him and they sat in silence. A lone bird swooped over the lake, the moonlight catching its wings. The stars stretched above, twinkling and sparkling like precious gems in the midnight black sky. Peace wrapped around her and she felt like she was right where she belonged. She liked this feeling of belonging in Sweet River Falls. Of belonging right here at Zach's side.

Not wanting to break the spell but knowing they both had to get up early for work, she finally turned to him. "I guess I should go in."

She was rewarded with a look of disappointment on his face. He sighed. "Yes, I guess so. It's getting late."

He stood and reached down a hand to pull her to her feet. She could keep that hand in hers forever...

But, he released her hand and helped her fold up the quilt. She hugged it against her, acutely aware that she no longer had his warmth against her. They walked over to his truck and he stood by the door.

"I guess I'll see you tomorrow?" He still just stood by the truck without any movement to actually get in and leave.

"Yes, I'll be over at the lodge, I'm sure."

"Are going to stop by and see me?"

She was pleased to hear an eagerness to his tone. "Sure. I'll come by."

"Good." He smiled but still just stood there, close, right in front of her.

He was looking directly at her face. So close. *Was he going to kiss her?*

She wanted him to, didn't she?

Oh, yes, yes she did.

But to her extreme disappointment, he stepped back and climbed into the truck. "See you tomorrow."

She nodded then watched as he drove away. She pressed her fingers to her lips. She'd been so sure he'd kiss her. Maybe she'd read him all wrong. What did she know about dating anyway? She'd thrown away a year or so with Eric because it had been easier to see him than to break up with him, and those kisses had only been quick kisses on the cheek like you'd kiss a friend.

And to be honest, she'd never had a man who truly loved her. Certainly not Pete's father. That had been one huge mistake. Not a mistake that she'd had her son, but that Pete's father had been Bree's boyfriend at the time. They'd both cheated on Bree, and Cece still sincerely regretted that and was so glad that Bree had finally forgiven her.

She turned to go inside. Bree had left on a lamp but must have gone to bed. Which was fine with her, because she wasn't sure she wanted to answer Bree's questions about tonight. She wasn't even sure she knew how she felt right now.

Except she knew she'd wanted him to kiss her. She'd wanted that very, very much.

CHAPTER 9

Madeline Stuart burst through the door to the Feed and Seed in Comfort Crossing, Mississippi. She'd finally gotten out of the lease on her place in St. Louis. The landlord hadn't even charged her for breaking it early because he'd found another renter. And she'd turned in her notice at work. It was really happening. She was moving to Comfort Crossing and marrying Gil. Everything was falling into place. She couldn't wait to tell Gil.

Gil looked up from behind the checkout counter where he was waiting on Frankie Johansen, and a big grin spread across his face at the sight of her. "Maddy, you're here." He rushed out from behind the counter and swooped her up in a big hug and swung her around. When he finally set her down, he kissed her quickly.

Frankie cleared her throat, and a smile played at the corner of her mouth. Gil turned to her. "Sorry 'bout that." The disarming grin on his face didn't say he was sorry—not one bit. He turned back to Frankie and finished ringing her out. "There you go."

Frankie shook her head, but the slight smile said she hadn't minded the delay. "You two have fun. Stop by Frankie's tonight if you can. Dylan Rivers and Missy are playing."

"We'll try." Gil nodded.

Madeline waited until Frankie left Gil's store. "Guess what?"

"What? You missed me so much you couldn't stand it?" He threw her an impish smile.

"Besides that."

"I give up. What?"

"So… got out of my lease in St. Louis early. I turned in my notice at work and I've made arrangements to have my things moved down here in two weeks."

"Best news I've ever heard. I'm so ready for you to be down here all the time instead of this constant travel back and forth." He came back out from behind the counter and took her hand. "Now, if you'd just set a wedding date, my life would be complete."

"Well then, be prepared to be complete." She grinned at him as his eyes widened.

"Seriously?"

"Seriously. You know how we went to Sweet River Falls last summer with your Aunt Josephine and Paul and visited my cousins and saw the Brooks Gallery that Paul invested in?"

"Of course."

"Well… if it's okay with you. I want to get married there in Sweet River Falls. At the lodge. I know it's not very advance notice but… I want to be married to you." She grinned. "If the last weekend in June works with you, we're all set."

"I'd marry you anywhere and any time." He circled his arms around her waist.

"I've always wanted to get married there. Ever since my parents took me there as a little girl. I even told my mother I'd get married there one day."

"Then that's where we should get married. Sweet River Falls it is."

"We need to tell your Aunt Josephine and Paul. And your sister, Bella, of course. And Aunt Catherine…"

He tossed his head back and laughed. "Yes, we'll tell everyone. I'm thrilled to actually have a date set. I'm sure everyone will move their schedules around to make it happen."

"My cousins, Bree and Cece, are doing weddings there now. Bree is catering and Cece is doing the planning. I've talked to them like three times this week trying to get things arranged. I know it's short notice, but they said we could get married that weekend and well... I couldn't wait any longer. Did I mention I can't wait to be married to you?" She grinned again.

"Best thing I've heard all day."

"Besides, I'm kind of tired of staying at Rebecca's B&B all the time when I'm here. Even though it's lovely, it's still not... well, a home."

"My home is your home. Let's get this wedding done so you can move in with me as my beautiful bride." He pressed another gentle kiss on her lips.

Her heart did a little flip. He still made it hard to catch her breath when he held her and kissed her. She leaned her face against his chest. "I'm so very happy."

"As am I." He kissed the top of her head and held her close.

CHAPTER 10

Zach found himself looking up from his work way too many times the next day. Lunchtime had come and gone with no Cece bringing him a picnic lunch. He looked at his watch.

She'd said she'd drop by, and he'd hoped it would be at lunch so he could take a break without feeling guilty. Who was he kidding? He'd take a break anytime with her if she'd just drop by.

He was still ticked at himself that he hadn't kissed her last night. He'd wanted to. But he'd been unsure of himself, first date and all. Besides, he'd proven that he didn't really know women. What they wanted. He obviously did a poor job reading them.

But Cece seemed different. Open. Honest. At least that was what his gut was saying.

He dropped his pencil on the plans and stared out the opening that should already have a window. A long breath escaped him. Maybe he'd just wander over to the lodge for a bit. He should update Jason on the progress of the building, shouldn't he?

And who was he kidding now? He just wanted to see Cece. See her smile and her one cute dimple. Watch her eyes flash when he teased her.

He looked at his watch. Again. Yes, it was definitely time for a break.

"CECE, you've got a visitor. Out on the front porch." Nora popped her head in the office Cece was using at the lodge. Nora had given her the space there to keep her paperwork and meet with brides.

Zach. She smiled, jumped up from the table, and hurried out through the lodge to the porch. She took a quick look in a mirror on the wall and tucked a lock of hair behind her ear.

She pushed out through the door, her heart

fluttering with anticipation, a wide smile plastered on her face.

A smile that quickly turned into a frown. "Eric, what are you doing here?"

"Hey." Eric smiled at her. "I thought I'd come see the attraction of Sweet River Falls. Why you want to move here."

"Eric… I thought…"

"No pressure. I just missed you. Wanted to come see the place."

She closed her eyes for a brief second, trying to catch her bearings. She'd done her best to let him down easy. Maybe *too* easy. Had he not understood? "Eric… I thought we decided that things… that we wouldn't be dating anymore."

"But we could still hang out, right? We always had fun hanging out." His eyes were eager, and she felt like a jerk.

"I'm not sure that's such a good idea. I just… I mean, I care about you, but I don't have feelings for you. Not like that. I don't think it would be smart to still hang out. I don't want you to think—"

"You don't want me to think that you led me on for over a year?" Suddenly his face hardened, catching her off guard. "That I waited patiently and gave you time because you said you didn't really date much?"

She swallowed. She'd pretty well messed this one up. "Eric, I'm sorry. I am. I didn't mean for you to get hurt. I was always honest with you, though. I never promised anything."

"But you kept seeing me."

"I—" He was right there. It had been nice to have someone to go places with. But she'd thought it was more hanging out as friends.

"Eric, I'm sorry if you got hurt. That wasn't my intention."

"I thought this was just a little phase of yours to get out of your dead-end job in Denver. I was going to say I'd still come here on weekends to visit."

"No, I don't think that's a good idea."

His eyes turned an icy blue. "So you got a guy here? You've been cheating on me? I know that's kind of how you operate."

She stepped back as if he'd thrown icy water on her. "I think you should go."

"Right. I think so too." He reached out and grabbed her wrists, his hard fingers digging into her flesh, pulling her close to him.

"Eric, stop, you're hurting me." She tried to

tug her arms away. Her heart pounded and a flicker of fear surged through her.

He leaned in close to her ear and growled. "Once a cheater, always a cheater." He finally let her go, spun on his heels, and stalked off to his car.

She rubbed her arms and looked down in dismay at the angry welts he'd made. She watched as he sped away and all she could feel was relief.

Relief and a bit of leftover fear. Her heart thundered in her chest as she fought to catch her breath and settle her jangled emotions.

Zach whistled as he walked down the path toward the lodge. When he got to the clearing, he paused and frowned. Cece was standing on the porch with some guy. They were deep in conversation. He hung back by the trees and watched. He told himself he just didn't want to interrupt them, that was all.

But feelings of distrust welled up in him and he couldn't beat them back.

He watched, stunned when the man took

both of her hands, pulled her close, and leaned in.

That was enough. More than enough. He'd seen plenty.

He certainly didn't need to see some guy kiss her. He'd been played for a fool, again. Cece had left off one tiny detail about her life. She had a boyfriend. A boyfriend who she was cheating on with him. He spun around and strode down the pathway back to the worksite.

How could he have been so foolish? He knew better. He'd sworn off women. The only thing he didn't know was why hadn't he listened to himself? He chastised himself every single step of the way.

Women cheat. They do. And he obviously was a lousy judge of the female character.

Zach stormed around the worksite and his workers steered a wide path around him after he chewed one of them out for not cleaning up after himself and Billy for not wearing his safety goggles. He went into the kitchen area that he was using for a make-do office, sank onto the stool, and rested his head in his hands.

He heard someone walking through the building and looked up when Jason stood in the doorway.

"I heard you were looking for me."

Zach stood. "You didn't need to come all the way over. I just stopped by the lodge to give you an update. Things are going fine." Just perfectly fine. Shingles weren't here. Windows weren't here. And the woman he thought he liked had a boyfriend.

"You okay? You look... funny."

"Just distracted." And angry. And if he was honest with himself, he was hurt a little bit. Which was ridiculous because he barely knew Cece.

Thank goodness his sanity had prevailed last night and he hadn't kissed her. He shoved away the thought that he'd just been *ruing* the fact he hadn't actually kissed her.

They both turned at a sound in the doorway.

Cece.

The last person in the world he wanted to see.

Standing there with an expectant smile on her lips. Not that he was looking at her lips. His whole body stiffened.

"Hi. I know I said I'd stop by today. I was busy and just now broke free."

Right, busy with her boyfriend.

"I'm kind of tied up with Jason right now."

Jason smiled at Cece.

Fine, go ahead and smile at her. Be nice to her. Traitor.

"I should go. We can catch up later." Jason turned to leave.

"No, don't go. I have some things to go over with you." He scrambled to think of what he could talk to Jason about to make his lie legit.

Jason frowned. "We could do it later."

"Now's fine." He looked at Cece. "Now's not a good time."

He could see the hurt in her eyes, which was ridiculous. So much ridiculousness going around today. Why was *she* hurt? *She* was the one who was cheating. He'd swear he saw tears gathering in her eyes, but he hardened his heart. No way he'd be played the fool again.

"Oh, okay. Well, I'll go then." She turned to leave and paused, giving him one questioning look over her shoulder, before turning back around. Her footsteps echoed through the building as she walked away.

CHAPTER 11

Cece had to fight back tears as she hurried out of the building. Zach had been so cold. Hadn't he said for her to stop by? After the whole ordeal with Eric, she'd wanted the comfort of being with Zach. To be honest, Eric had scared her when he grabbed her. She rubbed her arms where he'd grabbed her. The look in his eyes had been so… menacing.

Her first instinct had been to go see Zach. Talk to him, laugh with him. Feel safe.

But his face had held a disinterested look at seeing her, and his words had come at her cold and impersonal. His whole tone had said she was a bother, an interruption.

She determinedly fought off the tears, her emotions ping-ponging this way and that. Eric had upset her and so had Zach. Not in the same way, but they'd both surprised her.

She stood by the side of the lake, unwilling to go back to the lodge just yet, not wanting to see anyone. She needed some time to get her bearings. Picking up a smooth rock at the water's edge, she tossed it out onto the lake, watching it skip three times before it disappeared into the cold depths.

She'd thought that she and Zach had connected last night. She'd so enjoyed their time together. He was easy to talk to, funny, and his eyes mesmerized her. He was the first man she'd been interested in… well, in a very long time.

She picked up another rock and flung it across the water. This time it didn't skip, it just sank. Determined, she picked up another rock. That one refused to skip either.

With one last glare at the lake, she turned her back on it and headed back to her office at the lodge. Feeling sorry for herself wasn't going to get her job done.

She sat down at her desk and pretended to work.

Bree poked her head in. "Hey, I passed Eric on my way over here. He was speeding away in that fancy sports car of his. I looked for you, but couldn't find you."

"I was… I went on a walk." Tiny truth.

"So what did Eric want? I thought you guys broke up."

Cece stood, walked around her desk, and perched on the edge of it. "I thought we had, too. But evidently, I wasn't clear enough. He came here and said he would come every weekend to visit. It was like he hadn't even listened when I talked to him in Denver."

"So you told him again?"

"Very clearly this time."

"Was he hurt?"

She rubbed her arms and winced.

"What's wrong?" Bree stepped further into the room.

"He was angry, not hurt. Very angry." She glanced down at the angry marks on her forearms and unrolled her sleeve to cover them.

Not quite quick enough.

Bree walked over and pushed up her sleeve. "Did he do this?"

"He was mad."

"That doesn't give him a right to hurt you. Are you okay?" Bree hugged her, and her sister's arms were just what she needed. Or didn't need, because they broke through her every barrier she'd put up, determined to stay strong, and the tears started to flow.

"He scared me. The look in his eyes…" She swiped at the tears.

"I'm so sorry." Bree hugged her again. "At least he's gone now."

"Yes." Cece grabbed a tissue and dried her eyes. "He just caught me off guard."

"Why don't you knock off early and go visit with Zach?"

Cece shook her head. "I tried that… He said he was busy. He was—" She turned and glanced out the window, then back at Bree. "He was cold and distant. I don't know what's up with that."

"Why don't you talk to him and ask him?" Bree asked logically.

"Seriously, Bree… he practically dismissed me."

"He was probably just busy."

"Maybe." But Cece didn't really believe that. Something had changed. She was sure of it.

ZACH WAITED until dark before heading over to the lodge. He wanted to make sure Cece was long gone. He needed to run something past Nora or Jason. The doors they'd wanted were still on back order, and he'd found two new ones at a better price point that were available now, but he didn't want to order either of them without their okay.

He took a deep breath when he didn't see Cece's car parked near the lodge. Good. He was safe. He climbed up the stairs, and the door to the lodge opened and Cece stepped out.

He looked to the left and right, but there was no escape.

"Hey, Zach." She smiled at him, a tentative smile. "Do you... do you have time to talk?"

"I'm looking for Jason or Nora. Have you seen either of them?" Even he could hear how dismissive his tone was. Maybe she'd get the message.

She physically flinched. "I..." She took a step back. "They're inside. In the dining hall."

"Perfect. Gotta see them."

"Mom?"

They both turned at the sound.

"Petey—*Pete*—what are you doing here?"

Cece rushed forward and hugged the young man standing on the top step of the porch.

"My Friday class was canceled, so I came early to help with the wedding this weekend. Aunt Bree said she needed me to help serve."

Zach stood there staring at both of them. Her son? He looked at her and back at the young man. And back to her.

Another detail she'd failed to tell him. Another *secret*.

"Pete, this is Zach. He owns the company working on the new addition to the lodge."

The young man held out his hand. "Pleased to meet you, sir."

Zach stepped forward, shook his hand, and just nodded. He could barely speak. He didn't know this woman at all. And why had she kept her son a secret? Obviously, he knew nothing —*nothing*—about her.

Dodged a bullet on this one. For sure. For certain. He was *lucky* to find out everything before…

Suddenly he needed to escape. Far, far away from this woman. This woman and her son. The son she hadn't mentioned. "I better go, it's getting late."

"I thought you needed to talk to Jason or

Nora." Cece motioned toward the door into the lodge.

"It can wait until tomorrow." He turned and clambered down the steps and scurried—yes, that same ridiculous word—off to his truck. He climbed inside and couldn't help but glance back toward the lodge. Cece and Pete were nowhere to be seen. Which was a good thing, right?

He leaned his forehead on the steering wheel.

This had not been the day he'd thought he would have when he first woke up this morning all cheerful and full of hope.

Goes to show what can happen when a person has too much hope...

CECE LED Petey into the lodge and they went to the dining hall. "Come on, let's get you fed. I was just sitting with a whole group of us at the family and friends table."

Bree looked up and waved. "Hey, Pete. Didn't expect you until tomorrow."

"My Friday class was canceled because we had a test in the class Wednesday night."

"Well, sit down and let me run to the kitchen and get you some food." Bree started to stand.

Jason jumped up and put his hand on her shoulder. "No, you stay. I'll get something. Fried chicken okay with you?"

"Sounds great." Petey took a seat next to Bree.

Jason's sister Beth sat next to her husband, Mac, finishing up their meals. Cece sat back in the seat she'd vacated just five minutes ago when she planned to head back to the cabin. Now she plopped down, grateful for the diversion of having Pete here.

"I hear Nora put you in charge of getting things ready on the inside of the new building." Mac leaned back in his chair, his arm lightly resting around the back of Beth's chair.

"She did. I'm getting most of it sorted out. I still have to work out the arbor though. I could order one, but I kind of have a plan in mind. It will be portable, painted white, with trellises up the side." She'd meant to ask Zach to build it, but now she wasn't sure. Maybe she should just order one online. She could probably put it together herself if it came as a package. Not as special as she planned, but it would keep her from having to ask Zach for help.

"I could build it for you," Mac offered.

"He's great with stuff like that." Beth smiled at Mac.

Cece envied the easy way they were with each other. The happy glow of being newlyweds hadn't worn off yet.

"You sure you wouldn't mind?"

"Not at all. I'd love to contribute something to this new addition."

"I'll take you up on the offer, then."

Mac rubbed his chin then leaned forward. "I could stop by tomorrow afternoon and we could sketch out what you had in mind so I could get supplies."

"I'd really appreciate that."

"Then it's all settled."

And just like that, she found a way to avoid Zach. Avoid his cold voice and hard eyes. She didn't know what had flipped in him, but he'd made it perfectly clear when she'd asked if they could talk that he wasn't interested.

Fine. She wasn't interested either.

She wasn't upset. Wasn't hurt. Wasn't mad. Wasn't—

"Mom?"

"What?"

"I asked if it would be okay if Cody and I went hiking tomorrow morning. We'll be back in the afternoon to help with anything Aunt Bree needs."

"It's okay with me if it's okay with Bree."

"It's fine. It's supposed to be a nice day. Saturday though? I hope the bride won't mind moving into the lodge. I think it's going to be too stormy to have the wedding outside."

"Always a chance with outside weddings."

"Mom will be so glad when the addition is finished and she'll have that area to offer up if the weather is bad." Beth yawned. "I better go get the boys and we should head home. It's getting late. Mom has probably fed them enough cookies and ice cream that it will be a struggle to get them to settle down."

Mac and Beth got up. "I'll see you tomorrow."

"Thanks." Cece watched them walk away toward the kitchen, hand in hand. For the first time in a long time, she felt envy. For both of them. They'd found true love and they obviously enjoyed each other's company. She might never find that.

Not that she wasn't happy with her life. She

was. Eric had given her a good scare, and she was annoyed at Zach right now, but, all in all, her life was good.

And she realized she was switching over to being mad and annoyed instead of hurt. That was a good sign. She'd be fine.

She would.

CHAPTER 12

Nora poked her head into Cece's office again the next day. Cece held her breath, hoping it was better news than yesterday's surprise visit from Eric.

"I was wondering if you'd mind bringing this lunch over to Zach? I also have the choice picked out for new doors. He found a solution to our way-too-backordered doors we originally ordered."

She couldn't really turn down Nora's request, but she really, really didn't want to go over to the worksite.

"Something wrong?" Nora stepped further into the room and set the basket on the table. "I thought that you and Zach… I heard you'd gone out. Thought you might like a little break to go see him." She offered an encouraging nod of her head.

"We... we're not really going out. I don't know what is wrong, actually. He just turned... cold. And he's made it clear he doesn't have time for me."

"Men. They sometimes don't know *what* they want. That's okay. I'll run this over to him myself."

Cece pushed her chair back from the desk and stood. It was ridiculous to be chased away by Zach. She had every right to be over at the worksite. And besides, she needed to take another darn measurement that she'd been putting off getting so she could avoid him. "No, I'll bring it over. I have work I need to do over there anyway."

"You sure?"

"I'm positive. Besides, it's gorgeous out and a walk will do me good. Help me clear my mind."

"I don't mean to step in... but maybe you could talk to him? Find out what's wrong?"

"That's the sensible thing to do, but he just brushed me off when I tried to talk to him last night, then Pete showed up and Zach ran off."

"Maybe you could try again."

Cece got the impression it was more than a suggestion. Nora probably wanted them to get along so it didn't mess up anything with having the chalet ready on time. She reached for the basket. "I'll try. But I can't make him listen to me."

Nora grabbed Cece's shoulders, spun her around, and pushed her gently toward the door. "You'll find a way."

Cece stood outside on the front steps, trying to get up her courage to go confront Zach.

She sucked in a deep breath, clasped the basket tighter, and headed out to the path to the worksite. She didn't hurry on her way. It seemed like every little thing caught her attention. A cardinal singing in a tree. The way the sunlight glinted off the lake. A pair of ducks drifting along the water's edge. Even the puffy clouds above the mountains in the distance. She stopped to admire each sight and sound. Unfortunately, all too soon, she reached the building.

"Zach around?" she asked a young worker sawing some boards beside the building.

"He's inside, but I warn you, enter at your own risk. He's in some mood."

She straightened her shoulders and walked into the building. The sound of her steps echoed across the room. She paused at the doorway to the kitchen area, where Zach sat, his head bent over some paperwork.

She composed her face in her best version of I-don't-care and stepped resolutely into the room.

He looked up at her and there was not a hint of a welcoming smile, crushing any tentative optimism that yesterday she'd just been imagining things.

"Nora asked me to bring you lunch and her decision on the doors."

He nodded his head toward the end of the makeshift table.

And that silence with a dismissive nod was her undoing. "Seriously? You aren't even going to talk to me now? Do you want to tell me what it is that I did? We went out. I thought we got along. I enjoyed your company. I didn't know you were really such an—"

"*Seriously*, you're going to ask *me* what's wrong?" He stood quickly, knocking the stool over, and swiveled to face her.

"Yes, that's what I'm asking." She stood her ground, her heart pounding.

118

His face hardened into a mask that made him nearly unrecognizable as the Zach she knew. "How about the fact you have a boyfriend? You have to know how I feel about cheaters after what happened with my ex and my partner."

She lowered the basket on the ground. "I *don't* have a boyfriend. I told you that when you asked if there was someone special."

"So, someone special and a boyfriend are different things to you?" His eyes flashed.

"I don't know what you're talking about." Her forehead wrinkled as she tried to sort out what he was saying.

"I saw you yesterday. At the lodge. On the porch. You were talking and then he pulled you into his arms to kiss you."

What the heck? She drew herself up to her full five foot three and squared off with him. So that's what this was about. "So… did you think to ask me about it? You just saw me with some guy and jumped to conclusions."

"I saw him pull you into his arms."

Anger pulsed through her, and every fiber of her body throbbed with fury. She yanked up the sleeves of her shirt and thrust out her wrists. The angry red marks of yesterday had turned a nasty purple. "No, this is what you saw."

ZACH GRABBED hold of the edge of the table as he stared at the bruised welts on Cece's arms. "I don't—" He could barely choke out the words.

"Eric. You saw Eric. I did use to hang out with him in Denver. Nothing serious. I broke it off with him before I even came here. But—"

He watched her draw in a long, slow breath, but her eyes still flashed in fury.

"He came here to tell me we could do the distance thing. He'd come here on weekends. But I told him no. *Again*. He wasn't very happy with me. He grabbed me and…"

"He hurt you." His voice was low, and he tried to control his rising anger.

"I admit, he scared me some. But he's gone now." She started to roll down her sleeves to cover the bruises.

He took a quick step forward and took her hands in his, staring down at the bruises. "I'm so sorry. Sorry you were hurt. Sorry he frightened you. And I'm so, *so* sorry that I didn't just talk to you." He gently brushed a finger over one of the bruises with a whisper of a touch. He swore he could feel her pain and her fear from yesterday. He should have been there to protect her. He *could* have been there and none of this would have happened.

But, no, he'd hidden in the bushes. "I'm an idiot. I jumped to conclusions because of what happened with Felicity."

"I'm not Felicity."

"No, you're not." He brushed back a lock of her hair and tucked it behind her ear, looking right into her eyes. "I'm so sorry. Please forgive me. I was seeing what I thought was happening… and then… well, I didn't know you had a son, and that was quite a surprise, too."

"You didn't know about Pete?" A frown wrinkled her forehead. "I thought you knew about him. He's here a lot hanging out with Cody. Serving at the weddings. I just assumed you'd met him."

"So you weren't hiding him from me?"

She shook her head slowly. "No, I wasn't hiding him from you. I'd never do that. He's a big part of my life, even now that he's grown and away at college."

"I'm just so sorry…"

"So you've said." She tilted her head.

"I want to make it up to you. Can we start over?"

She stood there staring at him, and he was pretty certain she was going to toss him out of her life. He couldn't blame her.

"Under three conditions." She held up one finger. "One, no more jumping to conclusions."

He nodded.

She held up a second finger. "Two— talk to me if you have a question or you don't know what's going on. *Trust* me."

"And three?"

"Come over to the cabin tonight and I'll cook dinner for you."

Relief surged through him. "How about *I* cook for you instead? I owe you that much."

"I guess you do." She nodded slowly, then the corners of her mouth teased up in a grin.

"I'll pick you up at five?"

"I could drive over."

"Nah, I'll pick you up. My place is a little hard to find the first time."

"Five it is." She turned to leave. "You should eat that lunch Nora made."

"I should." Suddenly his appetite was back

and he no longer felt the urge to sit and break pencils.

"Bye." She slipped out of the room.

His heart lifted at the second chance he'd been given with Cece, and he swore he wasn't going to make another mistake with her.

CHAPTER 13

Zach left the worksite mid-afternoon—which he never did. He left Billy in charge and just hoped nothing came up to drag him back. He needed to shop for food and clean up his cabin.

He grabbed groceries and headed home. One road twisted into the next and he squeezed his truck through two boulders that really should be taken out, but no one on the road had really complained. There were only four cabins up here on this part of the mountain, and his was the last one at the end of the road.

He stepped out of the truck and grabbed the bags, pausing to look at the gathering clouds hovering over the peaks in the distance. They promised a heavy spring storm later this evening.

But he didn't care. Nothing could deflate his mood. He whistled as he entered the cabin and set the bags on a table by the door.

Okay, maybe *this* could deflate his mood a bit. He eyed the room.

Stacks of paperwork were scattered around. At least three jackets were thrown over the backs of chairs. A stack of unopened mail mocked him, and there had to be dishes from at least three meals piled on the coffee table—and he couldn't remember the last time he'd eaten at home. And not at the kitchen sink, for that matter.

He sighed and tackled the job.

An hour and a half later the place was picked up and cleaned. He'd started an easy soup from his mother's favorite recipe and made up a salad. Okay, it was a bag salad from the market, but still. It counted. He'd bought a loaf of bread and some ice cream. Nothing fancy, but a decent meal. He opened a bottle of red wine to breathe.

Then he looked down at himself, covered in dust and grime. Yes, he'd have to fix that too.

He took the world's fastest shower and pulled on clean jeans and a chambray shirt.

With one last look around the place, he pulled the door shut and headed to the truck. Thunder rumbled in the distance and he glanced at the sky. He'd better hurry and get Cece and get back here before the rains came in.

CECE PACED BACK AND FORTH, waiting for Zach. Bree, Cody, and Pete had headed to the lodge for dinner. She wished they were here for a distraction if nothing else. How many times had she paced this floor?

She could see the storm drifting in across the mountains. Looked like they were in for one of their famous spring downpours. She heard him pull into the drive, grabbed her jacket, and headed out to the truck.

He was just rounding the vehicle when he saw her. A wide smile spread across his face. That was more like it. She'd been almost afraid she'd see that cold, unwelcoming look again. She wasn't yet confident of her footing with him.

"I was coming to get you." He walked up to her.

"I figured we needed to hurry to beat the storm." Her words came out in a breathless rush of nerves.

He held the door open and she climbed in, acutely aware of how close he stood to her. He walked around and climbed into the truck. They headed out of town and into the mountains. "My place is on this side of Enchanted Peak. It's kind of isolated. Killer view though."

Silence dropped around them and she ignored—pointedly—how close he was to her, within arm's length. If she only had the nerve to reach out and touch him. She turned away and watched the scenery out the window. It never ceased to amaze her, the beauty of this area. So close to Denver and smog and the city life. But so very different.

They drove along in silence as he wound his way up the mountain. "You're right. I would have had a hard time finding you."

"Right, left, left then the left, right, left." His lips curved up in an impish smile. "I had to memorize that chant when I first bought the place so I'd know which forks in the road to take.

Cece thought this was maybe the fourth or fifth road they'd taken, splitting left, then right, then… well, she couldn't exactly remember. Maybe he could leave breadcrumbs for her if she ever drove herself.

"You're fitting through there?" Her eyes widened at two huge boulders sitting on each side of the road.

"Yep." He pulled through it like it was no big deal and plunged down the other side when the road swung down into a glen before heading back up the mountainside.

He finally pulled in front of a good-sized log cabin with a huge porch wrapping around it.

A flash of lightning followed by a loud crack of thunder reverberated through the truck.

"We better hurry before it dumps on us." Zach jumped out and came around to help her out.

She slipped down and stood for a moment in his arms. Her breath caught and Zach didn't move. She tilted her head up toward him as he leaned closer.

A loud explosion of thunder made her jump, and a yelp escaped her lips. She bumped her head on his chin.

He laughed and rubbed his chin. "Come on,

let's go inside." He took her hand in his, and she thought she'd be fine with just leaving it there all night...

Cece looked around the cabin as Zach switched on lights. Simple furnishings and windows with no coverings gave the room a homey feel. A quilt draped over the back of a worn brown leather couch. A stone fireplace with a stack of firewood rose up between the two-level windows stretching across the back of the cabin.

She gasped when she walked to the windows and saw the view. "My goodness, this is the most spectacular view."

Zach walked up behind her. "It is. I found this property and saw this view and just had to build this cabin, with these windows pulling it all in."

"You built this?"

"I'm a builder, remember?" He gave her a small smile.

"I know... but the place is gorgeous and... I love it."

"Thanks." He beamed at the compliment.

"Make yourself comfortable. I'll check on dinner. Glass of red wine?"

"Sounds wonderful." She watched as he crossed to the kitchen area. The whole kitchen and main area of the cabin were open and took advantage of the fabulous view. His attention to detail was evident in every aspect of the cabin.

He walked back and handed her the glass of wine, raising his own. "Cheers."

"To watching a spring storm roll in." She clinked her glass to his.

They stood in the window and watched the magic and power of the storm. Lightning flashed one after the other with rumbling and crashes of thunder. Rain lashed down, and small nuggets of hail started bouncing off the planks of wood on the deck. The overpowering force of the storm left her awestruck.

"It's a doozy." He moved closer to her.

"It is. I feel like I'm right in the middle of it all being so high up on the mountain." The electricity of the storm—or maybe it was just whatever was going on between them—made her jumpy, and she hoped she didn't scream again with another clap of thunder.

"I love living up here on the mountain. It's like a whole different world. So connected to…"

He shrugged. "Everything? Nature? The universe?"

It did make her feel part of something that was bigger than just herself. "I could probably stand here for hours and stare out these windows."

His rich laughter filled the room. "I *do* stand here for hours."

"I can see why you said you stand and eat at your kitchen sink." She nodded toward the kitchen area. "You look right out at this view."

"Yep, when I was designing the kitchen, I knew I wanted the sink on an island facing the view."

She stiffened when a flash of lightning hit close enough to shake the cabin and large hail began to bounce off the deck.

He stepped closer and put his arm around her waist. "We're safe in here."

She leaned against him, and for a moment it felt like they were the only two people in the world. He reached for her glass and took it from her. With a few quick steps, he placed the glasses on a nearby table and returned to her side. This time he took her into his arms, pulling her close. He took a quick inhale as if he was surprised at himself. He looked directly into her eyes, a speculative look on his face, as if deciding what to do next.

She held her breath and tried to hear over the pounding of her pulse. He leaned closer and reached out to touch her cheek with the merest featherlight stroke.

"Ah, I think I've been wanting to kiss you since the moment I met you." His voice was a throaty whisper.

The storm raging outside had nothing on the storm raging inside of her now.

His eyes glistened with desire and he touched her lips. "These."

The oxygen had emptied from the cabin because she could not breathe. Could not think. Could not do anything but stare at his face.

He leaned forward and brushed a kiss against her lips, and the range of sensations rushing through her almost made her knees buckle. She held onto his arms to steady herself as he kissed her again and deepened the kiss.

When he finally pulled away, a bemused expression rested on his face. "I—that— ah, that was—" He shook his head.

She gave him a tentative smile. "It was, wasn't it?"

He chuckled. "It was."

He pulled her against him, and she rested her cheek against his strong chest. His heart beat in an erratic rhythm that for some reason comforted her. She didn't want to be in this chaotic storm of emotions by herself.

"Cece?"

"Hm?" She didn't want to pull away to answer him.

"I'm really glad we worked things out."

"Me, too."

"So no more surprises?"

"I'm an open book. Just talk to me."

He tightened his arms around her, but somehow it felt gentle and strong at the same time. He stroked her hair and they just stood there like that. For how long? She hadn't a clue.

CHAPTER 14

He held her against him, afraid to move, afraid to break the spell. His emotions ricocheted through him. He wanted to pull her even closer, but he was so afraid he'd hurt her. He'd been especially careful to avoid her forearms, not wanting to cause her pain. Anger flashed through him at the thought of that Eric guy doing that to her. If he ever saw the guy, it wouldn't be pretty. His emotions bounced back to the peacefulness of holding her close.

His phone rang and he wanted to ignore it, but it might be something to do with the job. How the heck did a cell phone signal get through in this weather anyhow? He let go of her with one arm and snatched the phone from his pocket.

"Zach, this is Bob from down the road."

"Hey, Bob, everything okay?"

"Well, yes and no. No one is hurt, but we've had a rockslide at that old gully above my house. The road is covered."

"Did it damage your house?"

"Nope, just the road. Thought I should let you know. I've already called someone to shovel it out. But we're probably two-three days out from it being all cleared. Looks like you'll need to hike out until we can get it cleared."

"Okay, thanks for letting me know." He slipped the phone back into his jeans.

"What's wrong?" She looked up at him, concern in her eyes.

"Road's out. Rockslide. Looks like we're stranded here. We can hike out in the morning. There's a meadow down the mountain, and I'll have one of my workers meet us there to pick us up. It's a pretty steep hike though and a narrow trail at the first part."

A look of—something—crossed her face. Uncertainty? *Fear?*

"I'm sorry. I shouldn't have brought you up here in a storm. Of course, I had no idea we'd have a rockslide." His words came out rushed, trying to reassure her. "I guess you'll need to spend the night because we sure can't hike out in the dark and in this storm. But I have a guest room. I'll get it fixed up for you. I've got clean sheets for it somewhere. It will be fine. I'm so sorry."

Her eyes clouded and he'd *swear* he saw fear. She wasn't afraid to stay here with him, was she? Maybe she was skittish after the whole Eric thing. He rushed to reassure her again. "It will be okay. Hazards of mountain living, I guess. I promise. I'll get you out of here first thing in the morning."

"I know it's not your fault." She pulled away from him, uncertainty still etched in her expression. "So how about some of that dinner you promised me?"

And just like that, the magic was broken.

And try as he might, he couldn't get it back again. Not through dinner, not after dinner when they sat on the couch for a while. He held her hand, but that was all.

CECE LAY in bed in the guest room at Zach's cabin. She could hear him still walking around, but she'd begged off, saying she was tired. And she was tired, but that wasn't the reason she was so edgy.

Hiking.

He wanted her to *hike* out of here.

She used to love to hike. Get up in the mountains. Find isolated waterfalls and lakes. See such wonderful views from the mountain tops.

But she hadn't been on a hike since—she sucked in a quick breath—since the accident. Since Peter had died in her arms after he'd slipped on the hiking trail. The beginning of the whole downfall of their family, until by some miracle things had worked themselves out, albeit twenty years later. Bree had forgiven her for sleeping with Peter. It had been a terrible mistake. But one she hoped was way behind them now.

But hiking? She wasn't ready for that. She wasn't. She couldn't. Fear surged through her even though she tried to tell herself she was being silly. They were just going to walk down a path and get in a car and be back in town.

Easy. Simple. It would be fine.

Though he'd said the first part of the trail was narrow...

She rolled on her stomach and punched her pillow. She could do this. She could.

But hours later, long after she'd heard Zach go to bed, she sat up in bed and pulled the flannel shirt he'd given her to sleep in close around her. She stared out into the darkness out the window. The storm had subsided, and she only heard occasional rumbles of thunder in the far distance.

Maybe she was imagining it, but the shirt smelled slightly of Zach with a clean, fresh, outdoorsy scent that hovered around him. She pulled the collar up and rubbed it against her cheek.

Such a night it had been. Those kisses. Such magic. She reached up and touched her lips, wishing he was back kissing her again.

But all that had shattered when she'd started to freak out about the hike down the mountain.

She hated being so frightened, but she couldn't seem to talk herself out of it. She leaned back against the pillows and tried to convince herself it was time to sleep. But she sure didn't seem to be listening to her self-talk tonight.

CHAPTER 15

Zach got up at first light, trying to be quiet so he wouldn't disturb Cece. He pulled on jeans and a flannel shirt but padded around in his socks to mute his footsteps. He reached for his wallet from the dresser and knocked a book on the floor. It landed with a loud thud.

So much for being quiet.

He listened but didn't hear any noise from the guest room. Maybe she was a deep sleeper. He headed to the kitchen to make them coffee. He at least was sure about that. She did drink coffee.

He glanced at his watch an hour later after two cups of coffee himself. Still no noise coming from the guest room. He hated to do it, but he needed to get into town and get to the job site, so he went to knock on her door. "Cece? You awake? It's going to take a bit to hike down and I've got to get to work."

"Yes, okay." Her words came out muffled. "I'm sorry. Guess I overslept. I'll be right out."

Cece soon came wandering in the kitchen looking tired but adorable. He handed her a cup of coffee, and she wrapped her hands around it and pulled it to her as if accepting a precious gift. "Thanks."

"I called Billy and he'll meet us at the bottom of the mountain."

"Can't we just hike out the road?"

"It would be hard to get up and around the rockslide, and even if we could get around it, the road is about eight miles. This way down is only about a mile or so." He frowned. "Is something wrong?"

A long sigh escaped her lips. Not that he was staring at her lips because he so wanted to kiss them. "No, I'm just tired. Didn't sleep well."

"I'm sorry," he said automatically.

"I don't have hiking boots."

"What size shoe do you wear?"

"Six and a half."

"My sister leaves a pair of boots here for

when she visits. She loves to go hiking. She's got tiny feet like you. Let me check."

He walked down the hallway and looked in the hall closet. He moved boxes around and poked in its depths until he found them. He pulled out the boots and checked. A seven. He walked back and found Cece staring out the window.

"Success. These should be close enough."

She turned to him with the weakest smile imaginable. "Sure, that will be great. Let me just finish this cup of coffee and I'll go finish getting ready and we can leave."

Sure to her word, they were walking out into the morning sunshine within fifteen minutes. The air was fresh and crisp, and the leaves and rocks scrubbed clean from the storm last night. An earthy aroma tinged with pine surrounded them. "It's this way." He pointed to the left.

She nodded and they headed to the start of the trail. He led the way, dropping down between a stand of aspens and onto a faint trail. She followed close behind him. The path quickly got narrower with a long drop off on the edge. Her hands clutched at him her fingers white, grasping his forearm.

"It's okay." He placed his hand over hers.

"I've hiked it a million times. Looks scarier than it really is."

He frowned when he looked at her face. A green ashen color had covered her cheeks, and deep furrows etched her brow as she looked over the edge and down the steep incline.

"You okay?"

"I—" Her eyes flashed with fear. He could see that clearly now.

"You afraid of heights? Don't look down, then. Here, I'll hold only your hand. We'll be fine." He coaxed her forward.

She took a tiny step.

"Come on. The steep part isn't very long, then it's a pretty little trail down through the meadow."

She took another step, her eyes wide.

"That's right. You got this. Just look down at your feet, not the edge." He kept his voice low and soothing. They advanced about halfway through the steep part of the trail.

She took another step and her right foot slipped in the wet dirt on the trail. She lurched into his arms. "I can't. I can't."

He pressed her against him. "Sh, it's okay. I didn't know you were afraid of heights. I'm sorry. I'm so sorry." How did he not know this?

And why had he gotten her into this situation? Now they had no choice but to keep going.

She trembled against him and he stroked her back.

"The good news is we're about halfway through this. But that means either going back or forward, we still have to deal with it. So, let's finish going down the trail. Okay, this is how we're going to do it. You're going to be right at my side, on the inside edge and we're going to finish the hike."

"You'll be too close to the edge." Her eyes were wild and tears threatened to spill. Her breaths came out in little gasps.

She must be really, *really* frightened of heights. That would have been good knowledge to have before getting halfway down this trail, but this sure wasn't the time to bring that up. "It'll be fine." He tucked her against him as close to the inside edge as he could get her and they took a few steps. He concentrated on squeezing them down the narrow pathway, making sure he didn't make a misstep. He was pretty sure she couldn't handle that.

Finally, the pathway widened, and they dropped down into an easy trail among the trees. He could hear her breathing easing, though she still clung to his arm. "See, piece of cake. We're good."

"Don't ever, *ever*, do that to me again." She let go of his arm and stalked away, down the gentle trail.

He shook his head, uncertain exactly what it was that he'd done to her, and followed along behind her.

CECE RUSHED INTO THE CABIN, hardly taking time to say goodbye to Zach when he dropped her off. Bree walked out of the hallway and into the great room. "Good morning. I got your text last night that the road was out. Was wondering when you'd get home." She paused. "You okay? You look like you might be getting sick."

"I—" She gave up trying to fight it, and a trail of hot tears rolled down her cheeks.

"Oh, Cece, what's wrong?" Bree rushed over and wrapped her arms around her. "Did you guys have a fight?"

"No... we..." She gulped for air. "We had to hike out this morning."

"Hike?" Bree's eyes narrowed.

"Yes, the road was blocked, and it was the

only way out. Only part of the trail was so narrow." She closed her eyes, a vivid picture of the trail etched in her memory. "And I slipped. And it was awful. So awful."

"I'm so sorry. Come on, go sit at the table. I'll make you some chamomile tea. It'll help you settle your nerves." Bree headed toward the kitchen.

"I was so scared I could barely move." Cece still stood where her sister had left her. Bree came back, took her hand, and led her to the table.

After she put the teakettle on, Bree returned to sit at her side. "So… you haven't hiked since… since Peter, have you?"

"No. Not once. The most I've hiked is walking around the lake a bit."

"You used to love to hike." Bree patted her hand.

Cece looked down at their two hands. Bree's comforting, hers trembling. "I did use to love to hike. But after Peter died, I threw my hiking boots away. I vowed to never hike the mountains again. Besides… I'm so, so frightened of those narrow trails now."

"Did you tell all this to Zach?"

"No." She bowed her head.

"You should tell him, you know. It never works to keep secrets from those you care about."

"I—can't. I don't want to get into all that past history. The whole story of… Peter."

Bree squeezed her hand. "You don't have to, but I think it would be a good idea."

"Zach thinks I'm afraid of heights. I'll just leave it at that. I don't really want to explain… everything. And I certainly don't want to relive it again."

"Okay, you do what you think is best. But I still think if you two are going to be a *thing*, you should explain it to him." The teakettle whistled and Bree got up and went to make the tea.

"I just can't. And I'm not sure we're going to be a *thing* after I freaked out on him."

"So you didn't have a good time last night?" Bree brought two cups of tea back to the table and sat down.

"I did. It was great at first." She dunked her tea bag up and down. "He—he kissed me."

Bree grinned. "Well, of course he did. He likes you."

"I thought he did. I mean… his eyes were so intense and he seemed genuinely interested in me."

"Of course he is, silly. Who wouldn't be?"

"Well… no one has been, really. No one has looked at me like he did. Like he wanted me. Like he… *liked* me."

"You deserve to be liked. To be loved. And not some let's-just-hang-out thing like you had with Eric. Anyway, he proved himself to be a creep."

"To be honest, I want what Beth and Mac or you and Jason have. He adores you. You two are friends, too. Talk about everything. And the way he looks at you… you're one very lucky woman."

"I am lucky. I admit that. But, Cece, you can be too. If you just let yourself." Bree took a sip of her tea.

She wasn't sure. Wasn't sure she deserved a love like that. Not after what she'd done to Bree by going out with Peter. Having Peter's son. Maybe the universe was just giving her the karma she deserved. One brief hour or so of bliss with Zach… then it all had come crashing down. And he'd seen her at her worst on that trail, frightened and crying.

She shoved her hair behind her shoulder and took a sip of tea. She set the cup back on the saucer, trailing a finger along the edge. "I love this teacup. I think it's one of my favorite ones in Mom's collection."

Bree's mouth curved, easing into a smile. "You can change the subject if you want, and I know that's your favorite, that's why I made your tea in it. Thought it might cheer you up. Why don't you finish your tea and go grab a nap? You looked exhausted."

"But there's so much work still to be done for this weekend's wedding."

"And I'll do it. You get some sleep. Come on over to the lodge after you wake up."

She felt like she could go to bed and sleep straight through until tomorrow, but she'd set her alarm and only catch a quick nap, so she could get up and help Bree.

Her sister carried their teacups to the kitchen. "And I better not see you until way later in the afternoon."

Mind reader. Couldn't hide a thing from her big sis.

CHAPTER 16

After the hike down the mountain, things were different between him and Cece. Not bad, just not as good. He saw her off and on. They'd even gone to Antonio's again, and he'd kissed her goodnight when he dropped her off. He still couldn't get her warm, sparkling eyes and single dimple out of his mind. Thoughts of her were his constant companion. But he still didn't see her as much as he wanted because he was in an all-out panic to get the building finished in time.

He sat at another makeshift table, this time out in the main part of the lodge. Workers were in the kitchen installing the appliances and the stainless steel counter. He'd finally gotten a door for the kitchen along with the windows for that part of the building. Unfortunately, the large picture windows that were supposed to line the side of the building facing the lake were lost somewhere between the supplier and here.

He leaned back from the table and stretched. He'd hoped that Cece would stop by today. He wasn't sure what had changed that day of the hike, but something had. He'd asked her. Asked her twice. But she assured him nothing was wrong, she was just afraid of heights and embarrassed about her freak out.

Though he got the feeling it was something more. He just wasn't sure what.

Nora walked into the building sending appreciative glances all around. "It's looking great." She held out one of her infamous picnic baskets. "Feeding you. I know you rarely leave this place."

"Just trying to wrap things up." Like windows and shingles and some things that couldn't be finished until the windows were in.

"You still think it will be ready in time for Madeline's wedding?"

"Planning on it." Even if it killed him.

"So, there's a festival in town this weekend."

He grinned. "Of course there is."

"May Festival. You should ask Cece to go with you."

He bit his lip, tapping his pencil on the table, thinking. Maybe that was a good idea. Maybe it's just what they needed. They could go and have some mindless fun. And it wouldn't be anywhere near any heights or spooky drop-offs…

"I'll ask her. That is a good idea. I bet we could both use the break."

Nora smiled a self-satisfied grin, her mission complete. He wasn't sure the prodding him into inviting Cece wasn't the real purpose of her dropping by, even more so than the lunch.

She set the basket on the table. "Great. I'm going to try and sneak away and go, too. I love browsing the shops on Main Street and seeing everything all spruced up for the festival. It's like the perfect opening for the summer season here."

She left and he attacked the lunch. Two hearty sandwiches on homemade bread, some chips, orange wedges, and a large slice of pecan pie. He was sure going to miss this let's-feed-the-builder thing on his next job.

CHAPTER 17

Nora and Annie walked along the pathway between the Sweet River and the buildings lining Main Street. The festival had brought lots of tourists to town, as usual, and the path was crowded with people enjoying the festivities and the gorgeous weather.

"At least this year I'm not worried about rushing to finish the loft in time for the festival." Annie grinned.

"Last year when Nick showed up bringing Henry, the inspector, just in time to save the day." Nora smiled. "He's a good man."

"He is and I'm very lucky."

Nora loved seeing her friend's face light up when she talked about Nick. All Nora wanted was for Annie to be happy, and finally, she was.

They walked on, arm in arm, until they reached the courtyard area. Sophie Brooks was going to make a surprise appearance and sing a few songs in the courtyard before she and Chase did a benefit concert at the arena in town tonight.

They stood along the edge, waiting.

"I hear Sophie is going to sing a few songs, just like old times before she became so famous singing with Chase." Nora looked up to see Gloria Edmonds standing before them. How had Gloria found out? It was supposed to be a surprise.

"Oh, don't look like that. There's not much that goes on in this town that I don't know." Gloria gave them a Cheshire grin. "Like I heard that Walter Dobbs got the zoning committee to approve the sale of his land and okay it for putting in a condo development."

Nora sucked in a breath and Gloria plastered a superior I-know-everything look on her face.

"When did that happen?" Annie's eyes narrowed, and she looked at Gloria like she didn't believe her.

"Yesterday."

"There wasn't a notice about the meeting." Nora frowned.

"Oh, it was just called at the last minute." Gloria's eyes flashed with pleasure. "They had a quorum, so Dobbs brought it up and it passed."

"They can't do that." Annie shook her head.

"It appears they can if three-fourths of the committee and the mayor agree to it."

"I—" Nora closed her mouth, unwilling to give Gloria the satisfaction of seeing how upset she was.

"It's great news, isn't it? We'll finally get to have some condos built on that lake. Next up is seeing if we can get the lake zoned for motorboats and jet skis."

"That will never happen." Nora couldn't help herself, the words just erupted from her.

"Of course it will. It's time for the town to get with the times. It will bring lots more people to town. Everyone wins."

Except for people who prefer the quiet and beauty of Lone Elk Lake just like it is.

"Well, I better go. I'm not really interested in hearing just Sophie sing. I do have front row tickets to hear Chase at the concert tonight, though."

With that, Gloria walked away.

"I really don't like that woman." Annie glowered at Gloria's retreating back.

"Nor do I." Nora sighed. She had her work cut out for her to try and prevent this whole catastrophe from happening to her beloved Lone Elk Lake.

CECE STOOD near Annie's shop, waiting for Zach. She'd come early with Bree and had already walked around for a good half an hour, poking her head into some stores and watching the crowd of people mill around Main Street. The street had been roped off to cars. Booths of food, crafts, and local products lined the center of the street.

But she stood at their assigned meeting place precisely at noon like they'd planned. She spied him walking up the sidewalk in his normal confident stride, and a flutter took over in her chest. She needed to get over herself and get them back on solid footing. She'd just been so embarrassed and upset about the whole hiking incident and had refused to talk to him about it, even though he'd asked. Finally, he'd seemed to get the message that it was going to be a non-topic. She hoped it stayed that way. She just wanted to forget the whole thing.

He saw her watching him and lifted a hand in a wave as he threaded his way through the crowd. He finally reached her, with a smile that seemed to be just for her.

Okay, time to turn this around.

She gave him a hug, and surprise widened his eyes, but he held her close for a moment before releasing her.

Nice, they were off to a good start.

"What do you want to see or do first?" he questioned, his hand still lightly resting on her arm.

"Well, if it's up to me to decide... let's go down by the courtyard area. I heard there's a funnel cake vendor down that way."

"Ah, feeding the sweet tooth. Excellent way to start the afternoon." He took her hand and they started down the street, stopping here and there to browse around booths that caught their fancy.

They shared the delicious and oh-so-sweet funnel cake. "You've got a bit of powdered sugar there." He touched the side of his mouth.

She swiped a hand across her face and

grinned. "They are messy, but one of my favorite indulgences."

"I'll remember that. Along with sopapillas." He took her hand again. "Now what? You know, now that the important part of the day has been accomplished."

She grinned. "Walk around some more? There's still brats, or hot dogs, oh, and ice cream. We need ice cream. Oh, and fudge."

"All that?"

"At least. What good is it to go to the festival if you don't overindulge?"

"Indeed, what good is it?"

Bree and Jason strolled up to them with his sister's boys, Trevor and Connor. Bree glanced at Cece's hand clasped in Zach's and smothered a smile, but not quick enough for Cece to miss it. "Hey, you two. Did Cece get her funnel cake yet?"

"She did," Zach answered.

Trevor tugged on Jason's hand. "Can we go to the game area? I wanna see if I can win a prize."

"The prizes are stupid." Connor rolled his eyes at his younger brother.

"Are not." Trevor's eyes clouded.

"I'll go with you. I love to play the games.

I'm pretty good at the ring toss." Zach smiled at Trevor.

"See, he's an *adult* and *he* likes the games." The boy puffed out his chest. "Even big people like the games. Everyone likes the games. And the prizes are *not* stupid."

They all headed to the game area, and even Connor grudgingly played some of the games. Zach won a baseball cap at the ring toss and gave it to Trevor. The boy tugged it onto his head, backward, and there it remained for the afternoon.

Cece watched Zach's easy manner with the boys. Defusing the brotherly spats, encouraging Trevor when none of his rings hooked on the stakes, all the while paying attention to Connor's efforts too. This was a side of the all-business-all-the-time Zach that she hadn't seen.

He threw his head back and laughed at something Connor said and the boy grinned in response.

Trevor grabbed her hand and tugged her down so he could whisper in her ear. "Miss Cece, Zach is cool. You can bring him to play anytime."

"I'll remember that." She smiled at the boy.

"I told Mom we'd meet her at Annie's shop.

We should probably head back that way." Jason rounded up the boys and he, Bree, and the boys headed down the street.

Cece stood by Zach's side watching them walk away, Trevor jumping over every crack in the sidewalk. She glanced at Zach and saw an amused look on his face. She stood up on tiptoe and kissed his cheek.

"What was that for?" The smile in his eyes sent her pulse racing.

"I just… you were great with the boys. And I'm having a great afternoon. And the weather is perfect. And I love this town. And… well, thanks for inviting me." Her heart was full of pure happiness and contentment.

"My pleasure, ma'am." He sent her an impish grin that did nothing to calm the storm raging inside her. "How about I go get you that hot dog you were wanting? Or ice cream?"

"Ice cream sounds good."

"Of course it does. What flavor?"

"Butter pecan if they have it. If not, vanilla. Or chocolate. Surprise me."

He grinned and hurried off in the direction of the ice cream vendor.

She leaned against the brick wall near the courtyard waiting for her treat.

"There you are."

She whirled at the sound of Eric's voice. "Eric." She searched the crowd for Zach or Bree or anyone she knew.

"I thought you might be here at the festival."

"What are you doing here?" She stepped sideways putting more distance between them.

"I came to apologize. I lost my temper the other day. I want to work things out with you." He gave her a boyish please-forgive-me look or maybe an it-wasn't-really-my-fault look.

She wasn't fooled. The bruises had faded, but she hadn't forgotten them. Her heart pounded and she folded her arms in front of her. "Eric... no. There is no working things out."

His eyes glittered with the same mean streak she'd seen the last time, but then quickly changed to righteous innocence. "Of course we can work things out. Don't be silly. It was just a little lover's quarrel."

"We were never lovers." She searched the crowd again. She knew so many people here in town, where were they when she needed them? "And it wasn't a little quarrel. I want you to leave and not come back."

"Listen, Cece—" He grabbed her wrist, and

she choked back rising fear as she tried to tug her hand away from him.

She looked left and right, fighting panic.

"Let go of her." Zach's cold, hard voice came from behind her.

"Walk away, mister. This is a private conversation."

"I said to let go of her."

"This the guy you cheating with?" Eric's angry eyes flashed at her but she still couldn't break free of his grasp.

Zach stepped in front of her and pried Eric's hand from her wrist. "I think you should leave."

"I think you should mind your own business. Cece and I are having a discussion."

"Eric, I want you to leave."

"You heard the woman." Zach's voice held a threatening, commanding tone.

Quick as lightning, Eric swung at Zach. Zach caught his arm mid-swing. "I don't think we need that here at the festival." His voice was calm, rational... and cold as a glacier.

Eric yanked his hand away. "You can have her. She's not worth it anyway. She'll just cheat on you like she always cheats on people. You can't trust her." Eric spun around and disappeared into the crowd.

She struggled to breathe over her pounding heart that seemed to fill her whole chest and sank against the brick wall again.

Zach looked closely at her, his eyes filled with concern. "Are you okay?"

She nodded.

"You sure?" His forehead wrinkled.

"I'm sure. But I've never been so glad to hear your voice." She gave him a weak smile.

"I was standing in line to get your ice cream and looked back and saw him standing there and... well, I couldn't get over here fast enough." He looked down at her wrist. "There's going to be bruising again."

She rubbed her wrist. "Probably."

"I'm sorry I wasn't here to stop it sooner."

"I'm just glad you showed up when you did. Hopefully, he got the message this time."

Bree and Jason came hurrying up to them. "Cece, are you okay? I just saw Eric, and he looks spitting mad. We left the boys with Nora and came to find you."

"I'm okay. Zach saw him and came over and... well, I think Eric is gone for good this time."

Bree hugged her. "I'm so sorry he keeps showing up. Hope this is the last time."

"It better be." Zach's eyes were stormy dark with held back anger. He leaned against the wall beside her and draped an arm around her shoulder. She leaned against him, protected and safe. She finally took a deep breath and relaxed. Or at least she tried to.

ZACH DID his best to control the anger that surged through him. He didn't want to upset Cece any more than she already was. A strong wave of protectiveness coursed through him and he kept an arm around her shoulder as they wandered around the festival for a little while longer.

"You look tired." In truth, she looked like she would fall off her feet. The encounter with Eric had obviously and justifiably worn her down.

"I am a bit."

"I'm going to take you home."

She nodded.

He drove her home to the cabin. "You going to be okay?"

She glanced at him, her eyes weary and a look of hesitation on her face. "I— I don't really want to be alone. Bree was going to have dinner with Jason tonight. Could you… could you stay for a while? Eric has me so… unsettled."

"Of course I'll stay. As long as you want me to."

He walked her inside, and she walked over to the window, staring out at the lake.

"Cece, can I get you anything?"

"I—no—yes." She scrubbed her hands over her face and squared her shoulders. "Yes, let's take a glass of wine and go sit on the swing and watch the sunset. I'm tired of… well, I just want to relax."

She carried a quilt held against her while he carted the two glasses of wine outside to the swing. He sat beside her and she dropped the quilt onto their laps. He handed her a glass, and she took a small sip, savoring the flavor. "Ah, that's what I needed. A good red wine. My dad's swing. A pretty sunset."

He settled an arm around her shoulder and pulled her close. She leaned against him and a small sigh escaped her lips. They sat in silence with the gentle motion of the swing calming her. Calming him. He kissed the top of her head and she looked up at him and smiled.

Still, they sat in silence.

The sky erupted in oranges and yellows and a streak of purple arched above the mountains. "That is so beautiful. This view here on the lake never ceases to soothe my soul."

"It is very peaceful here," he agreed.

She looked up at him again. "Thanks for staying. For being here."

"There's no place I'd rather be." And there wasn't. He wanted to be right here by her side. And even with the Eric incident today, they seemed to have found their way back to an even footing, and he was very grateful for that.

One lone star blinked in the deepening sky. "First star. Make a wish." Cece pointed to the heavens.

"I really don't wish for anything right now. You wish." At this very moment, he had all he could have hoped for and he was perfectly content.

She closed her eyes and a serious expression crossed her face. She opened her eyes and smiled. "There. I made a wish."

"What did you wish?"

"I can't tell you or it won't come true."

"Well, we can't have that happen, can we?" He took her hand in one of his and balanced his wine glass against his knee with the other. They continued to swing gently as the evening swathed them with its calm darkening skies.

A handful of stars began twinkling above them, then more and more as the sky turned an inky dark blue.

"I should probably go in now and let you get home." Cece turned to him.

"I said I'd stay as long as you wanted."

"I'm okay now. I am." Her voice sounded more like she was trying to convince herself then convince him.

"I think we should just sit here a bit longer." So they did. He took her empty glass and set it and his gently in the grass beside them. He turned back to her and placed a finger under her chin, tilting her face up to his. He looked questioningly at her and she nodded slightly. He lowered his lips on hers, finally, finally getting the chance to kiss her again. It seemed like an eternity had passed since he'd kissed her like this. A mistake he didn't plan on making again.

He finally pulled away, and she looked up at him, a bemused expression on her face. "I've missed those kisses."

He gave a low laugh. "Me too, woman. Me, too." So he kissed her again in the magical starlight.

CHAPTER 18

The next day Zach went to look for Cece at the lodge. Tomorrow was supposed to be gorgeous weather, and he hoped to play a little hooky and convince her to do the same.

She looked up from her desk as he stood in the doorway. A smile spread across her face and warmed him and made him very happy they were in this better place now. Back in sync.

"Hi." Her eyes sparkled with pleasure.

He stepped into the room. "So, I was thinking. Tomorrow is supposed to be a gorgeous day. I thought I'd try to convince you to play hooky with me. Take the afternoon off."

"What did you have in mind?" She stood and walked around her desk and right up to him. Close. Inches away.

What had he been saying? He had no clue.

He leaned down and kissed her, one hand circling the back of her neck to pull her closer. He lost all thought of his grand idea. She finally pulled away and smiled at him. "So the plan? What do you have to entice me away?"

"What?' Oh, his hooky plans. "I thought we could go on a hike." He rushed to explain when he saw her eyes start to cloud over and she took a step back. "Not a hard one with steep drop-offs, just an easy one, up over the ridge by Grace's Peak and down to Lost Lake. It's an easy trail. No heights, no drop-offs." He knew that area well and had specifically chosen that trail because of how easy it was, but it was also very beautiful.

"I—I can't." She stepped back behind her desk. "I'm really too busy. I need to help Bree, and I still have things to finish up with the chalet."

"You could take a half day. I'm sure Bree wouldn't mind."

"I can't." Her words were sharp, and he looked at her in surprise.

"Okay, I understand." But he didn't. Not really. She'd been pretty okay with the idea of taking time off until he'd asked her to go on a hike.

"I better get back to work." She settled onto her desk chair.

"Okay, yes, I should get back to work, too. I'll see you later."

She nodded, and he left the office, feeling adrift and once again not sure of his footing with the woman. How did this keep happening?

He headed down the pathway to the job site, his mind racing, turning over possibilities of what he'd done wrong. Just last night... everything had seemed perfect between them. He'd kissed her in the moonlight. Kissed her a lot. Everything had seemed better between them.

But now? He paused and stooped to pick up a smooth stone from the water's edge. He tossed it into the lake and watched the ripples spread across the water. Ripples. Every action, every decision, had ripples. He raked his fingers through his hair, exasperated. He didn't know what decision had caused this ripple.

"If you were trying to skip that rock, you failed." Jason walked up to him, picked up a small stone, and skipped it across the water.

"What's up? You have on what my mom calls a thinking face."

He let out a long stream of breath. "I don't know. Women. I'll never figure them out."

Jason laughed. "Truer words were never spoken. I take it this is about Cece? She doing okay after the run-in with Eric?"

"I think so... or thought so. I went to go ask her to join me in playing a little hooky tomorrow afternoon."

"Good choice. Supposed to be a perfect day weather-wise."

"So she seemed to agree with the idea until I suggested we go on a hike. Not a hard one. I know she's afraid of heights. But then she said she couldn't go."

"Of course she won't. She hasn't hiked in over twenty years." Jason looked down and kicked the dirt with the toe of his boot. "Uh... she's not afraid of heights. She's afraid of *hiking*. Hiking trails."

"Yes, she is. I saw it firsthand when we hiked out from my place after the rockslide blocked the road."

Jason bit his lip. "It's a bit more complicated than that."

"If you'd clue me in, I'd sure appreciate it."

"It's really Cece's story to tell." A pensive look crossed Jason's face.

"Well, she's sure not telling it to me. Please, tell me what's going on."

"I'll tell you the gist of it, but then ask Cece, okay?"

He nodded.

"You met Pete, her son?"

"Yep."

"His father, Peter, was killed in a hiking accident. He died by slipping off a trail, and it wasn't a hard trail either. Just an unlucky misstep."

"Really?" He frowned.

"Cece was with him. Saw him trip and fall over the edge. She scrambled down the ravine to him somehow—I'll never figure out how she did that—and she was sitting with him when he died." Jason looked out at the lake. "Peter was my best friend. I miss him. He never even got to meet his son."

"I'm so sorry." No wonder she'd been so frightened on the way down from his cabin. "But, why wouldn't she tell me this?"

Jason shrugged. "The rest of it is hers to tell or explain."

Zach held out a hand. "I appreciate you

telling me about this. I don't want to push her to do anything she's not comfortable with."

Jason shook his hand. "No problem. I just thought you should know after you said she'd turned you down. I sure wish she'd at least try some easy trails. We used to all go hiking when we were younger. Had so much fun. Bree and I still do. But Cece refuses to join us, even on easy hikes."

Too bad he hadn't thought of a much better idea for tomorrow afternoon. Like a picnic by the lake—no trails involved. He had to pick the one thing that she was never going to do...

"I'd better go. Mom's got a long to-do list for me. We're still scrambling to make sure everything is ready for Madeline's wedding."

The wedding. He really should get his mind back into the job. "I'd better go, too." They headed out in different directions, but Zach still had a hard time concentrating on anything but Cece.

CECE LOOKED up to see Zach standing in the door to the office yet again. It better not be another invitation to go hiking...

"Cece, can we talk?"

She wanted to say she was too busy—and she was—but avoiding things wouldn't solve anything. She stood, pushing the chair back. "Okay."

"Let's go take a walk by the lake, what do you say?" His eyes questioned her.

"Sure." It appeared all she could think of was one-word answers.

She followed him out of the lodge, and they walked along the shoreline until they got to a big boulder jutting out on the edge of the lake. He sat on it and she dropped down next to him.

"So, I thought we had no more secrets, no more surprises." His voice wasn't really accusing, just, questioning.

"What do you mean?"

"I asked you to go on a hike and suddenly you didn't have time to spend with me tomorrow."

"I said I was busy…" But her excuse sounded fake, even to her ears.

"Listen, Jason told me about Peter."

Her breath caught and heart began to pound. He didn't. He couldn't have. It wasn't his to tell. She looked at Zach, searching his face, looking for the inevitable sign. It was coming. He was going to break up with her because he'd found out about Peter. He'd never trust her now that he'd found out. And who could blame him?

"He told me about Peter's accident. How you were with him when he died." ~~Jason~~ Zach took her hand. "I'm so very sorry. Such a tragedy that he never even got to meet his son. You must have been heartbroken."

"I—"

"I wish you would have told me. No wonder you were so freaked out on that ledge when we had to hike out from my cabin. I'm so sorry." He squeezed her hand. "But we don't need secrets. You don't have to hide your fear from me."

She closed her eyes, willing her heart to settle.

No more secrets. No more surprises. She sucked in a long breath and looked him directly in the eyes, getting lost for a moment in the warm depths of his sparkling blue eyes. Eyes filled with understanding.

Only he didn't understand.

Not all of it.

"Zach, there's more to the story."

"So tell me the rest." Those understanding

eyes encouraged her.

She drank in the warmth and acceptance of those eyes for one last time. Because he was never going to look at her the same after she explained it all to him.

"It was a terrible time. I'd just found out I was pregnant, and I told him about the baby while we were hiking. He was so surprised. And then he slipped…" She struggled to find enough strength to go on. "I was with him when he died. The park rangers finally found us and got us out. But he was… he was already… gone."

"I'm so sorry. It must have been so frightening for you."

She held up a finger. "That's not all."

"Okay." He searched her face.

"Peter… Peter was Bree's boyfriend."

"I don't understand." A frown settled on his face.

"I slept with Peter while he was dating Bree. It was a mistake, both Peter and I knew that right away. But, clearly not soon enough."

"You slept with your sister's boyfriend?" She didn't miss the disbelief in his tone.

"I did. And I'll regret it for the rest of my life. Except, I don't regret having Pete. Not at all. It was the one good thing that came out of it."

"But you and Bree seem so close."

"That just happened recently. We barely spoke for over twenty years. She avoided anything having to do with our family. It tore our family apart. Though that's all on me, not her. I can't blame her. But this last year we worked things out. She's forgiven me."

"For cheating with her boyfriend?" Skepticism flooded his eyes.

"She has. I don't know how she has, but we've worked past it. Our boys are good friends now. And… well… we have our family again. I just wish we could have worked it out before my parents died. My mom would have been so happy."

He sat in silence, but he'd dropped her hands. Her cold, empty hands.

"I know you have a thing about people cheating. I know what Felicity and your partner did. How much that impacted your life. I just… I'm sorry. I can't change my past, though. But I'm not the same person. I was really young. And stupid. And, well, I don't really have an excuse."

His phone rang, breaking the silence, and he

took one long look at her before snatching his cell from his pocket. "Hello." He turned to look at the lake while he listened. "Okay, I'll be right there." He pushed off the boulder and stood, brushing off his jeans. "I've got to go. Problem at the job site."

"Zach, wait..." She reached out for his hand, but he shoved it in his pocket.

"I'm sorry, I've got to go and... I need some time." He turned around and headed toward the chalet.

She sat on the cold stone, staring out at the lake. She wouldn't allow herself to cry. Not now. Not this time. It was all her own doing. She'd made that mistake all those years ago with Peter, and it haunted her life to this very day.

CHAPTER 19

Bree was doing dishes at the cabin when Cece got home. "Hey, I thought you might be going out with Zach tonight."

"That's not going to happen." She leaned against the counter.

Bree turned off the water and dried her hands on a towel. "What do you mean?"

"I'm pretty sure we're broken up for good this time."

Her brows shot up in surprise. "But I thought—"

"Right. Me, too. But that was before I told him about Peter."

"You told him… everything?"

"Everything. And he just… walked away. But who could blame him? He hates cheaters.

He's always been clear on that." Her shoulders slumped and despair swept through her.

Bree walked over and leaned against the counter beside her. "Maybe he just needs a little time. He cares about you. It's obvious."

"Maybe. But cheating is the one thing he can't forgive. I can't blame him. I've ruined it. But it's my fault. I deserve this for what I did." She stared down, noticed the bruise on her wrist, and tugged on her sleeve to cover it.

"You don't deserve this and you're not that same young girl."

"I'm not. But... I did cheat and I can't change that. And I'm pretty sure that's the one thing he can't forgive. He'll never trust me now." She'd made so many mistakes.

"Then he's a fool." Bree hugged her close.

"I'm at least glad things are good between you and me now," Cece whispered as she leaned against her, taking in her older sister's comfort and strength.

"Things are good between us and I'm very grateful for that," Bree agreed.

Cece didn't have the energy to move, so she didn't. Not even after Bree went over to finish the dishes, then headed to her room. She didn't like the hopeless feeling that settled around her, but no matter how hard she tried, she couldn't chase it away. She felt like she'd been so, so close to getting what she wanted, and it had all been snatched away. And it was her own fault.

But at least she'd told him the truth. No secrets.

Zach tried to concentrate on the job at hand. Check the invoices and make sure they matched up to what they'd actually received at the job site. No matter how many times he ran the numbers, they didn't match. Not from one vendor. So it definitely was *his* error, not a true problem with the orders.

He did know where the real problem was. It was the fact that he'd fallen for a woman he didn't know if he could trust. Something he'd sworn he'd never do again. Granted, she'd been much younger when she'd had the affair with Peter... but it instilled this doubt in his mind. A doubt that dug at him and prodded him to back off.

His life was probably too busy for a girlfriend anyway. That one lonely thought didn't do much to comfort him. He sighed and took another stack of invoices, determined to match them up with the proper orders.

"If you aren't the biggest fool in Sweet River Falls."

Zach looked up from his desk to see Jason planted directly in front of him. "What?"

"I talked to Bree. I heard that Cece told you the whole story about Peter."

He scowled. Why did everyone need to know about his relationship with Cece? "She did."

"And you just walked away? Didn't talk things out?"

"I got called back here. I've got a job to do. My first priority."

"Your first priority should never be work over people you care about." Jason challenged him.

"But—"

"No, hear me out. Women like the Stuart women don't come along every day. Smart, funny, talented, hard workers. Not to mention they are both beautiful. And you, my friend, are a fool."

"So you've said," he said wryly.

"Cece made a mistake. A mistake over *twenty years* ago. She's never forgiven herself, even though Bree has forgiven her. We make mistakes when we're kids. It's life. She's been paying for the mistake for a very long time. She was just starting to make peace with it... and you're screwing that up."

"Me?"

"Don't you see? If you walk away from her now because she told you the truth... she'll just use it to punish herself again."

"I didn't mean—"

"Don't let your hang-up about Felicity and your business partner ruin a good thing. Cece is not Felicity. She's a great woman. Kindhearted. And if you break her heart... well, that's on you. She was honest with you. You do what you need to do... but walking out on her now will crush her."

A heavy weight pressed against his chest. He hadn't meant to hurt Cece. He'd just... been... *afraid*? Nah, he wasn't afraid, he just couldn't deal with someone cheating on him again. He needed to *trust* them. He looked at Jason standing there glaring at him.

"Maybe you're just too scared to take a leap of faith. Too scared to risk your heart. She's worth it, you know." Jason turned to leave but glanced back. "And as I said, you're a fool if you let this mess things up between the two of you."

He sat there for a long time after Jason left, mulling over his words. Maybe Jason was right, he'd been a fool. He was *still* being a fool. Was he going to let his fear destroy what he had with Cece? What he *wanted* with Cece?

He jumped up from the table, knocking the stool over in his haste. He hurried out of the chalet and off to find Cece.

He didn't want to be a fool for one more minute.

CECE SAT on the swing by the lake, unable to get motivated to go over to the lodge to work. Or maybe she was just making sure she'd avoid Zach. She was certain it would crush her to see him again. She needed time to get herself together and find a way to hide the pain. She'd hoped the swing would bring her some kind of comfort. She trailed her fingers over the well-worn wood, but still, she couldn't find the energy to get up and do something. Anything. Anything but sit here and feel sorry for herself.

She turned at the sound of someone approaching and her breath caught in her lungs.

"We need to talk." Zach stood in front of her, not asking her, but telling her.

"It's okay. I understand. I don't need you to spell it out for me. You can't trust me, and trust means everything to you." She swallowed and glanced to the left, trying to avoid looking at him.

He sat down next to her, and it took all her power not to scoot away from him. His familiar fresh, outdoorsy scent surrounded her, and she wanted to escape it. Escape this one last confrontation.

He took her hand, and she looked at him in surprise. "Look, it's my hang-up about Felicity. Jason ever so kindly pointed out to me that I'm being a fool." He looked right into her eyes. "And I am."

She sat there in silence, stunned, letting him speak.

"I'm sorry I walked away. It was wrong. I just—I know my baggage with Felicity and my partner is… well, it's *my* baggage, my problem. You're not like her. I know that."

She looked at him as sadness overwhelmed

her. He was giving her a chance. Giving *them* a chance.

And yet… she couldn't take it.

She'd never really know if he trusted her. And he probably wouldn't. It would always be a question in the back of his mind. She couldn't do that to him and didn't think she could do that to herself either.

"So, we can go back to how things were, okay? Before I was a fool." His eyes pleaded with her.

She sat there, looking into his eyes, searching for the right words. "Zach… no. You'll never truly trust me. I don't want you to have to live like that. With that always hanging over our relationship. I've made my mistake and I'll live with it. But you don't have to."

"No, it's not like that."

"But it is. It will always be there between us."

"I can work with it. I'll get over it." He squeezed her hand.

She pulled her hand away from his. "You shouldn't have to deal with it or work with it. I just want you to be happy. Not in a relationship that you'll always question."

"It won't be like that." He shook his head.

She stood. "I know it won't because there isn't an *us*. There isn't a relationship. I can't forgive myself for what I did, so why should you?"

He looked at her for a long moment, his eyes filled with sadness. "Or maybe…" He hesitated. "Maybe you're afraid of forgiving yourself. Afraid to take a chance on being happy."

His words bit into her with their hint of truth.

But it was what it was. She'd never been able to forgive herself, and she wasn't going to put him in the middle of a relationship where he'd always have doubts. She turned and walked back to the cabin, her heart breaking, leaving him sitting alone on the swing.

But certain she'd made the right decision. For him. For them.

CHAPTER 20

A week later Cece walked around the loft area of the chalet. She'd made sure Zach was away from the job site before she'd trekked over there. She glanced around the area, visually picturing the finished loft in her mind. They could use this area, with chairs, if the bride had a larger wedding. Everything had been planned so well on this design. The flooring up here was reclaimed wood, rich in color and worn to a luminous patina. The area had been stair-stepped up so anyone sitting up here would have a view of the arbor below in the main area.

The workers still needed to finish the front railing to the loft. They'd only put up a temporary rail. But this part of the chalet at least was almost finished. Well, except for the large picture window. The window had come with a crack in it, and Zach was waiting on a replacement. Or so she'd heard. Because he didn't talk to her. If he saw her come over to work, he headed the other direction. Not that she blamed him.

She sank onto a stack of boxes near the edge of the loft. The view *was* beautiful from up here, too. They were so close to finishing if something else didn't come along to ruin things. The last inspection was scheduled on the chalet, and Nora said that Zach assured her everything would be ready.

Madeline and Gil were due here in just a few days.

She should be happy. She'd done a good job for Nora on the venue. It was going to be a lovely place to get married. Mac had finished the arbor, and it was even better than she imagined. She looked down at the arbor sitting in front of the windows spanning the front of the chalet.

One of those windows was missing, too. She frowned. There wasn't much time, and she wanted it all to be perfect for Madeline.

The stairs creaked slightly and suddenly

Zach appeared in the loft. He looked as surprised to see her as she was to see him.

"Oh, I didn't know you were up here."

"I was just leaving." She stood, and a box she'd been sitting on crashed behind her.

He hurried forward and picked it up, glancing at the label. "Oh, no problem, nothing breakable"

"Sorry."

He set the box on top of the stack she'd been sitting on. She took a step away. "I should go."

He shrugged. "Don't let me chase you off."

"No… I…" A noise behind Zach made her reach out her hand. "The boxes—"

He whirled around, trying to catch them before they cascaded to the ground floor. She watched in horror as he lost his footing as he wrestled with the boxes. His arms flung wide as he struggled to catch his balance.

Time stood still. Peter's face and his sparkling blue eyes flashed before her as he tumbled over the side of the trail. Zach's stormy blue eyes opened wide as he struggled not to fall off the loft.

A scream escaped her, torn from her throat, raw and full of terror. "Zach!"

A loud cracking noise exploded through the air as the railing split. She watched in disbelief and reached out for him, to steady him, to catch him. But he disappeared over the edge, followed by an awful crash as he and the boxes hit the floor below.

She whirled around, not daring to breathe, and rushed down the stairs. Zach lay crumpled on a stack of smashed boxes. She cleared some debris to reach him. "Zach? Zach, are you okay?"

"I—" His eyes opened but fluttered closed again. "Not sure."

"Don't move." She scanned the area. No one was around. "Help. Somebody help."

No one answered. She reached in her pocket for her phone but realized she'd left it at the lodge.

"Help. Help us." It was all so eerily familiar. All alone with an injured person. No one around. Yelling for help. She closed her eyes briefly to chase away the memories. "Help us!" She yelled again. And again.

She brushed a lock of his hair away from his face and noticed the blood on his hair. "Sh, don't move. Don't move."

The sound of loud footsteps on the wooden floor drew her attention from Zach's ashen face.

"Oh, Jason, thank goodness. Call for help. Zach fell from the loft."

Jason grabbed his phone and dialed as he sank beside her on the floor. "Need an ambulance. At the lodge. Zach Berry has taken a fall. Not sure." He turned to her. "How long ago?"

Minutes? Hours? "I don't know." She panicked and looked at Zach. "Maybe ten minutes? I'm not sure."

"Ten minutes, maybe. He's kind of conscious, but not totally. There's blood on his head. No, we won't move him. Right. We're at the chalet job site. I'll get someone to meet you at the entrance to the lodge and direct you here." He clicked off his phone and redialed. "Mom, Zach's hurt. I've called an ambulance. Meet them at the entrance and bring them here to the chalet. Yes, Cece is here with him. Okay."

He dropped his cell phone and leaned over Zach. "You're going to be okay. I've called for help. Hang in there, buddy."

Zach's eyes opened briefly, and he opened his mouth.

"No, don't talk. Just stay quiet." She touched

his face as he closed his eyes again. She looked at Jason and could see the concern in his eyes.

"What happened?" Jason asked softly.

"I was up in the loft. He came up... the stack of boxes I was sitting on started to fall and he tried to steady them and lost his balance." She closed her eyes and felt Jason's hand on her shoulder.

"It's going to be okay. Help is coming. I'm here with you. It's going to be okay." His words were a litany of comfort as he tried to soothe her, but it wasn't working.

Flashes of Peter's fall and Zach's fall mingled and twisted in her brain. It was all she could do to take in breath after breath, her eyes on Zach's face, willing him to be okay.

Breathe. Breathe. Breathe. She timed her breaths to his jagged ones.

"Zach, please, please be okay." She whispered the words against his cheek as her tears fell on his face.

SHE SAT in the waiting room of the hospital.

The same hospital she'd sat at over twenty years ago when they'd brought Peter here. Only

Peter had already been dead when they brought him here.

Zach was not dead. She kept reminding herself.

Zach was going to be fine. He was. If only her thoughts could make it so.

When she'd come here with Peter, she'd known he was gone. She'd known that, but his family hadn't. She'd had to stop them as they rushed into the hospital, and she'd started to tell them what had happened.

But then she'd fainted.

She refused to give in to a fainting spell now. She would be strong. She looked down at Zach's blood on her shirt and wiped at it ineffectually with a tissue.

She jumped up from her chair and paced the waiting room. Jason sat leafing through a magazine but wasn't even pretending he was reading it or concentrating on the pictures in it.

She paced back to stand by Jason. "Do you think he'll be okay?"

"Sure he will." Though Jason's eyes didn't show the certainty that his words said.

"Cece." The familiar sound of her sister's voice broke her thoughts. Bree rushed over and wrapped her arms around her. "Are you okay?"

"I'm fine. It's… Zach."

"Nora called me and told me. I got here as soon as I could." Bree looked closely at her. "Are you sure you're okay? You look pale."

"I'm fine. Really." She wasn't, but—well, how she felt didn't matter now.

"Are you Zach Berry's family?" The doctor entered the waiting room.

Jason stood and walked over to him. "Zach's sister is on her way. He's the builder working at our lodge on the lake. This is Cece, Zach's… friend."

"Ah, that's who he's asking for. Cece."

"He's asking for me? He's awake?"

"He was. We gave him something for the pain."

"Is he…" She sucked in some air, but it didn't seem to have any oxygen in it. "Is he going to be okay?"

"He's one lucky guy. Dislocated shoulder that we're going to fix when the pain meds hit. No broken bones. Couple dozen stitches in his head. Possible concussion. We're going to keep him a day or so. And he's going to be pretty bruised up and sore for a while."

She started to crumble then, but Jason

steadied her. "He's going to be okay. It's all okay."

The tears started to pour in hot streams down her cheeks. For Zach. For Peter. For the relief she felt right now.

He was going to be okay. Zach was okay.

She turned to Bree. "Can you take me home?"

Her sister frowned but took her by the arm. "Of course. Whatever you need."

"You're not going to go in and see him?" Jason questioned.

"No… I…" She shut her eyes and slashed at the tears on her cheeks. She opened her eyes. "No. He needs to rest."

"But you're coming back when he's awake?" Jason stared at her and Bree shot him a leave-her-alone look.

"Come on, sweetie, let me get you home." Bree led her out of the waiting room, out of the hospital, out into the fresh air and sunshine.

Only, she still couldn't breathe.

CHAPTER 21

Cece slept fitfully all night, tossing and turning with dreams of people she loved falling and falling. She'd woken up with a start, again and again, her heart pounding. She finally gave up trying to sleep and went to go sit out by the lake, wrapped in a quilt. She watched as the stars began to fade and the sun began its magic, lighting up the sky.

Bree came to join her, pressing a cup of coffee into her hands. "You been up long?"

"A while."

"You going to head in and see Zach?" Her sister settled on the swing beside her.

"I—I don't know. I mean, we broke up and that hasn't changed."

"It could."

"Could what?"

"It could change."

"But he'll never forget what I did. That I cheated with Peter. It will always be there between us."

"Well, it's there between you and me, and we don't let it ruin things for us," Bree said matter-of-factly.

"And it took us over twenty years to get to this point."

Bree turned to face her. "It's like this, Cece. And listen to me carefully. You almost lost him yesterday. You deserve happiness. Someone who loves you. Zach does love you even if he doesn't realize it yet."

"No, he doesn't." She pursed her lips. Did he?

"He does. And you have to forgive yourself and realize that you are worthy of love. Worthy of happiness. Please, it's time to forgive yourself and move on with your life."

"I don't know if I can forgive myself." Her words were but a whisper.

"Then you're making the biggest mistake of your life. Bigger than the one with Peter. You're throwing away happiness because you're afraid to admit you deserve it. You've never been a coward, Cece. Don't start being one now."

Bree stood up and walked away and Cece looked out at the lake. No wind stirred the surface. The birds were silent. It felt like the whole world was waiting for her decision.

ZACH SLOWLY WOKE up the next day with the worst headache in the history of headaches along with every single muscle in his body screaming at him. He peered between slit eyelids and squinted against the light. A machine beeped. He glanced around the sterile hospital room as the memories slowly came back to him.

The fall.

He closed his eyes.

He started to reach up to touch a sore spot on his head, but his arm was trapped in a sling. He licked his lips, sure he was dying of thirst.

"Hey, buddy." Jason's voice made him attempt to open his eyes again.

"Jason." His voice croaked the word. "Water."

"Sure. Here." Jason held a glass of water and helped him with the straw.

The cool water soothed his parched throat. "Thanks." His voice still sounded like a scratched record.

"You remember what happened?" Jason offered him another sip, which he took gratefully.

He started to nod yes but quickly realized that was a mistake. He gritted his teeth against the pain. "A fall."

"You were lucky, though. No broken bones. Dislocated shoulder. A bit of a concussion. Some stitches in your scalp."

He swallowed as he tried to gather his thoughts. "Cece. She was there. She's okay? I saw her reaching for me…"

"She's fine."

He turned his head slowly—ever so slowly—to look around the room. "Is she… here?" He tried to hide how eager he was to see her.

"She was here yesterday. Bree took her home."

"But she's okay? She screamed and—"

"She's pretty shaken up. I think it was so similar to watching… to seeing Peter fall over the edge of the trail."

"I bet she's upset. It must have brought back all those memories. I'm a fool. I know how to be safe at construction sites. I just wasn't concentrating. I—" He smiled sheepishly. "She just throws me off balance. Literally this time I guess."

Jason grinned. "Next time, try not to do it so close to the edge, buddy."

"Good call."

"When does the doc say I can leave? I got stuff to do at the chalet to get it finished."

"Don't worry about it. If it's not done in time, it's not. Madeline and Gil will understand. We'll rethink their setup. Maybe try to have it outside." Jason gave him another sip of the coveted water.

"It's supposed to rain next week. That will mess up having it outside." Zach frowned. "Call the doc and see if I can get out of here."

"Forecast could change. And you're not leaving until the doctor says you're good and ready."

Zach settled against the pillow and closed his eyes. He needed to get to work. He did. But maybe he'd just rest his eyes for a brief moment.

~

Cece, Bree, and Jason sat at a table at the dining hall of the lodge that evening. Cece had steadfastly avoided going to the hospital. She was sure that was the right decision.

Certain.

Mostly.

Jason had asked her if she was going to see Zach, but she'd just given him a shrug as an answer.

Annie and Nick came in with Nora, and Cece welcomed the interruption. They came over and joined them at the table.

"I do love it when the friends and family table is full." Nora smiled as she sat down.

"I was too tired to cook, and Nick suggested we come here. I thought it was a great plan." Annie sat beside Nora, and Nick took a seat next to her.

Beth and Mac walked up. "Looks like everyone had the same idea tonight."

Nora motioned for them to sit. "This is even better. Both my kids here tonight."

They all ordered and chaos descended on the table. Dueling conversations and laughter. Cece remained quiet and just listened as the words flowed around her.

"So, is the chalet almost finished?" Nick's words caught her attention.

"Jason said that Zach is out of commission for a few days. I don't think he's going to get the chalet finished in time for Madeline's wedding." She knew that Zach must be devastated to not have the project completed on time, though it was out of his control now.

"What's left to do on the chalet?" Nick asked.

Jason leaned forward. "I'm not certain, but a couple of windows need to be installed. I saw they got delivered today. The railing on the loft, of course." He gave a wry grin. "And I'm sure there are other little things. The inspector, Henry, is scheduled for two days from now. I guess I'll call him in the morning and reschedule."

"Zach is going to be upset." Cece's heart tightened as if she could physically feel Zach's disappointment. Not to mention they had to figure a way to pull off Madeline's wedding without the occupancy permit on the chalet.

"I practically had to tie him to the bed to keep him at the hospital tonight." Jason shook his head.

"But he's going to be okay?" Annie asked.

"He is, in time," Jason assured her.

Nick rubbed his chin. "You know, I put myself through school doing construction. I'd be glad to help."

"And I helped my father with his construction company. I did a lot of the loft at Bookish Cafe. I'd be glad to help, too," Annie offered.

"I'm handy. I'll help." Mac joined in.

Nora grinned. "You know, I think with all of you helping, we might just pull it off."

"I'll talk to Henry—he's a fishing buddy of mine. Maybe he can run by and tell us what's left to be checked off his list." Nick's forehead wrinkled. "I think we can finish it up and give Zach a hand."

Cece looked at these people so willing to jump in and help Zach. Help get the chalet ready for Madeline's wedding.

And darned if tears didn't begin to flood her eyes. She'd cried more in the last few months than she had in her whole life before this. And she was ever so tired of tears.

She sighed. This town, these people, they were why she was so glad she'd moved to Sweet

River Falls. They were all willing to jump in to help Zach.

Bree looked at her with a questioning glance.

"I'm fine," she whispered as she choked back the tears.

CHAPTER 22

Z ach didn't care what the doctor said about
taking it easy. He was going to the job site.
He might not be able to get the chalet finished
by Cece's cousin's wedding, but he was going to
get it finished ASAP. He was so annoyed at
himself for missing the deadline. Fall or not, he
didn't miss deadlines. Ever.

He pulled his truck up near the chalet and
frowned. The area was crowded with trucks and
cars and a couple of delivery vans. He slowly
hauled himself out of the truck, ignoring his
aching shoulder, and headed for the chalet. He
walked through the doorway—which now had
two glass doors installed—and looked around in
surprise. The building was filled with his
workers and people from town.

Jason walked up to him and grinned. "Looking good, right?"

"What's going on?" He scanned the room, noticing the missing window along the lakeside of the chalet was being installed as they spoke. "How'd the window get here? They said it would take a week."

"Mac called the glass company, then drove into Denver to pick it up."

"But… all these people…"

"They're just here to help you out. Should be all finished by Madeline's wedding. Nick got the inspector to come out, and we got a list of everything that's required to be finished to pass inspection. You'll still have a few things to wrap up, but the chalet should be ready for the wedding."

"I don't understand."

"Well, Nick offered to help, and Annie. Then Mac said he would. Then Cece called around to get more people here. She's pretty persuasive when she puts her mind to it."

"She did that for Madeline?"

Jason rolled his eyes. "I'm thinking she did it more for *you*."

For him? But she didn't want anything to do

with him. She hadn't even come to visit him in the hospital.

"Anyway, aren't you supposed to be home resting up?" Jason eyed him.

"I'm fine."

"You're stubborn, I'll give you that. If you insist on being here, come sit down and I'll show you the list of what we're working on to get things finished up."

Zach looked around at the dozen or so people installing the window, hanging light fixtures, and putting the much-needed railing up in the loft area.

Jason nodded toward the loft. "Made a decision to install a half wall up at the edge of the loft, and a railing above the half-wall. Not taking any more chances. Henry okayed the plan change."

"I don't even know what to say." Overwhelming emotions ran through him. Surprise, relief, gratitude. "Jason, I can't thank you enough."

"Don't thank me. Thank Nick for suggesting it, and Cece for rounding up the workers."

CECE STOOD in the far corner of the chalet watching Jason and Zach talking. She wasn't really surprised to see Zach show up here even though, according to Nora, the doctor had told him to go home and rest for a few more days.

She wasn't sure Zach knew the definition of rest.

Zach looked her direction, and she knew the moment he realized she was standing there. He stopped talking and Jason turned to see what had caught his attention. Jason nodded his head her direction, and Zach started across the distance toward her.

She didn't know if she wanted to flee... or maybe meet him halfway.

She did neither, and he walked right up to her, albeit with a slow, unsteady gait. "I hear you got all these workers here to help finish the chalet."

"It was Nick's idea. He's got a lot of experience."

"Well, I'm grateful to all of you." He stood in front of her mindlessly rubbing his arm that was in the sling. "So... are you okay? I know I frightened you with my unfortunate... tumble."

"Tumble? That's one way to put it. And you

did scare me. But you're the one we've all been worried about."

"You've been worried about me?" His eyes brightened.

"We all have, of course."

A slight frown crossed his face. "I didn't mean to worry you."

"Zach, it's okay. I'm just glad you're okay. Well, pretty okay. I imagine you're still sore."

"I'm fine." His words said one thing, but she'd seen him wince when he shifted his arm in the sling.

"Why don't you sit down?"

He looked at her for a moment. "Yes, I will. Jason wants to go over some things with me. I just wanted to make sure you're okay."

"I'm fine." She mimicked his words, but she wasn't really sure she was fine. She was so grateful he was okay, but the scene played over and over and over in her mind. Zach plunging through the broken railing and falling to the ground below. She scrubbed a hand over her face to swipe away the memory.

"I'll get back to work then." He turned and headed back to Jason. She watched every step he took, looking for some reassuring sign that he was truly okay.

CHAPTER 23

"Who's the guy who can't take his eyes off of Cece?" Madeline stood in front of a full-length mirror, finishing getting ready for her wedding.

"That's Zach. He's in love with Cece. But she won't let him love her." Bree continued buttoning up the multitude of tiny buttons that trailed up the back of Madeline's wedding gown.

"Hey, you two. I'm right here." Cece looked up from where she was tugging on her shoes. They were cute, but really not very comfortable. She'd gotten used to everyday flats. She stood and wobbled a bit in the heels. Not good.

"So why won't she give him a chance?" Madeline picked up a necklace from the dressing table and draped it around her neck. Bree hooked it for her.

"I'm still here." Cece walked over to them.

Madeline looked at her in the mirror. "So why won't *you* give him a chance?"

"We just have some… stuff… that we can't work out."

"Every couple has stuff. Gil and I did. And we lived in separate cities half a continent away from each other. Relationships are hard work. But so worth it with the right person."

"And this Zach guy is the right person for Cece, she just won't believe it." Bree gave her an I'm-the-older-sister-and-I-know-this look.

"Cece you are a wonderful woman. But I swear, you just don't see it. You don't believe you deserve to be happy." Madeline scowled.

"That's exactly what *I* told her." Bree bobbed her head enthusiastically.

"You two can quit ganging up on me. And anyway, it's Madeline's day. Change the subject." Cece touched the necklace around Madeline's neck. "That's lovely."

"It was my mother's."

"It's beautiful." Cece admired the gold chain with the tiny heart and gold filigree clasp. She gave Madeline a quick hug, being sure to not mess her dress. "I know you miss your mother today."

"I do." She paused, obviously fighting back tears.

"She's here with you. I know she is." Bree stopped with the buttoning and stood beside Madeline. "You can feel her here."

"I just miss her so much." Madeline's voice was barely a whisper.

"I know, sweetie, I know." Bree put her arm around her shoulder. "But Cece and I are here for you. I'm sorry Abby couldn't make it."

"You're all the family I have left."

"But you're marrying Gil and will have all of his family now."

Madeline smiled. "And it's a great family to marry into. I love them all so much."

"Let's finish getting you ready and get you married then."

Bree tackled the last of the buttons, then Cece adjusted the beautiful headpiece entwined in Madeline's hair with a small, simple veil hanging down her back. They all stood and stared in the mirror.

"You look… beautiful," Bree said.

"Gorgeous," Cece added. "You ready?"

"I'm so ready." Madeline nodded.

~

Madeline stood beside Gil at the arbor covered in white flowers and twinkling lights. The cloudy gray sky outside the large picture window did nothing to dampen her mood. Everything was perfect. She was marrying the love of her life. Gil squeezed her hand, and she looked up into his shining eyes.

She glanced out at the people sitting here, sharing in their special day. Gil's Aunt Josephine and her husband Paul sat in the front row, holding hands like newlyweds. Which they kind of were after recently finding each other after years and years. His Aunt Catherine sat with Bella, Gil's sister. Bella's lifelong best friends, Jenny and Becky Lee, were here. They'd all practically adopted her as a BFF after she and Gil had gotten engaged.

Cece had been right. She was gaining a family. A very large family. She turned back to look at Gil. He mouthed the words "I love you" and squeezed her hand again.

The ceremony went by in a blur of I do's until Gil leaned forward and gently touched her face, then pressed a kiss on her lips. A good long kiss. Then one more.

Everyone erupted in applause and laughter. He took her hand in his, and they walked back down the aisle as husband and wife.

They walked outside to the large deck overlooking the lake and stood while people walked by to congratulate them. Gil held her hand and kept sneaking quick kisses, a boyish grin on his face each time he kissed her.

"You look beautiful." Bella walked up and hugged her. "So beautiful. I'm so glad to have you as my sister now."

Madeline hugged her back. "Thank you."

"I'm going to claim your cousins, too. I adore Cece and Bree. It's been great getting to know them." Bella moved on as more people stopped by with their congratulations.

As the people filtered away for drinks and appetizers, she finally had a moment alone with Gil. "I'm so happy." And she was, even though, a part of her longed for her mother's presence.

He touched her necklace as if reading her thoughts. "She's here with you, you know."

She reached her hand up and clasped the tiny, golden heart. Just then the sun broke through the clouds, and the sky lit up in brilliant shades of yellow.

"Oh." A lone tear trailed down her cheek. "She's here. Yellow. That's her favorite color."

"Of course she is." Gil gently kissed the top of her head as they stood and watched the sunset unfold.

CHAPTER 24

Cece sat in the swing beside the lake. She wanted to believe her sister and Madeline. That it was the right thing to do to give Zach a chance. To give *herself* a chance to find the elusive happiness she'd been looking for.

If only something or someone would give her a sign.

A lone red cardinal swooped past her and landed on a log near the water's edge. He turned his head to look at her. He hopped along the log, coming closer. He wasn't a bit afraid of her. Heck, he was braver than she was.

Braver than she was.

He hopped closer, cocking his head and staring at her.

"Hey there, Mr. Cardinal."

He sang her a short burst of chirps, looked at her one more time, and flew away to the branches of a nearby tree.

The sun burst out from behind the clouds, flooding the lake with golden light.

The cardinal sang again.

And suddenly she knew what she wanted to do. What she *needed* to do. She jumped up from the swing and saw Jason approaching her.

"Hey, Cece. I just thought you'd like to know…" He paused, looked down at his feet, then back up at her. "Zach is headed back to Denver. Said he'd pick up some jobs there in the city for a while. He wanted to give you some space and said it was just too da— *darn* hard to be here right now."

"He's leaving?"

"Yep."

"He can't." He couldn't. Not now. Not when she'd just made her decision. "I've got to go find him."

"He just headed back to his place. Said he had a pounding headache, and he didn't look so hot. I think he did too much, too soon. But he said he's leaving for Denver. I can't talk the fool into resting for a few days."

"Thanks for letting me know." She rushed

into the cabin and grabbed her purse. Panic raced through her. Had she waited too long to make her decision?

"Where you going in such a hurry?" Bree looked up from the table where she was sorting the mail.

"I've got to go find Zach."

"Well, it's about time." Bree nodded with a wide grin spread across her face. "About time."

Cece rushed out to her car and headed to Zach's. Now if she could just remember all the turns to get there. Was it right, left, left then the left, right, left. Or was it left, left, right then left, right, left? She started to drive past the meadow at the bottom of the mountain and frowned. What was Zach's truck doing parked at the meadow?

A man approached her from the trail leading out of the meadow and waved to her. "Road's out ahead. Rockslide."

"Again?"

The man peered at her. "You know about that? Are you Zach's girl?"

"I—" How did she answer that?

He didn't give her a chance. "Anyway, looks like we're going to have to put up a retaining wall. Zach and I've been hiking in and out the last few days."

He shouldn't be hiking up there after his fall. Was he crazy?

The man got into an SUV parked beside Zach's truck. "The trail's the only way in or out right now."

She pulled her car next to Zach's truck and turned off the motor. She'd just call him to come down to the meadow to talk to her.

She dug through her purse, found her cell, and called him. She let it ring, but he didn't pick up. Well, he couldn't leave with her sitting right here. Eventually, he'd have to come down to his truck. She'd sit here all night if she had to.

She frowned. But why wasn't he answering his phone? He got fine reception up there. She tried him again. No answer.

Jason had said Zach had a pounding headache. Was he okay? She drummed her fingers on the steering wheel.

She sat there for thirty minutes, calling him every five minutes or so. No answer. Her cell phone battery taunted her as it crept near zero percent. She dug through the glove box of the car, hoping she'd put in the charger for the phone, but no such luck.

Then the phone was dead.

A red cardinal came and landed on a tree right beside her car. He stared at her, cocking his head to the side. She'd swear it was the same one that had stared at her at the lake. But of course, it couldn't be…

He sang his song and hopped along the branch. He gave her one more long stare, then swooped off through the meadow and disappeared up the pathway.

Her pulse began to race as she looked across the meadow at the trail disappearing between the pines. She got out of her car and looked both directions as if expecting help to come. She could hike up the road… but how would she get around the rockslide? Zach had said the terrain was steep near the slide.

She slammed the car door without thinking about how frightened she was. Without thinking about the trail. All she could think about was Zach.

She headed off at a brisk pace along the gentle incline of the trail through the meadow and threaded her way through the trees. She stood at the bottom of the steep part of the path and looked back behind her at the gentle trail leading back to safety.

She sucked in a deep breath and put one foot on the trail ahead of her. Then another. She kept her eyes on the path as she crept along, refusing to look at the edge, refusing to do anything but concentrate on one step after the next.

Step, breathe, step, breathe. She concentrated on the rhythm of the words. Step, breathe, step, breathe. Her foot slipped, and she caught herself by grasping a rock on the inside edge of the trail. Her heart pounded, and she closed her eyes, frozen in place, too scared to move forward.

Then she thought about Zach. Not answering his phone. Jason had said Zach wasn't feeling well. The stubborn guy had done way too much since the accident.

She slowly opened her eyes, still staring at her feet, and willed them to move.

Step, breathe, step, breathe.

Then she looked down, darting her eyes to the edge of the trail, and realized the path had widened and she was heading through the trees at the top of the trail. She quickened her pace and rounded the top of the trail and climbed on the road by Zach's cabin.

She rushed over to the cabin and knocked on the door.

No answer.

She hurried around the deck of the house and stopped short when she got to the back deck overlooking the mountains. Zach sat on a chair, staring at the view, lost in thought. The panic she'd felt began to abate. Some.

"Zach."

He looked up, his eyes wide with surprise. "Cece?" He jumped up and crossed the distance between them. "What are you doing here?" His forehead creased. "*How* did you get here?"

"Up the trail, of course." She said it like it was the most logical answer in the world.

"But—you don't do trails."

"I do when you won't answer your phone and I'm worried sick about you being up here and hurt."

He frowned and reached into his pocket. "Must have left the phone inside in my bedroom."

She wasn't sure if she wanted to smack him, hug him, or….

She threw her arms around him. "I'm so glad you're okay."

"Ouch."

"Oh, sorry. Your arm." She stepped back.

He stood there with a puzzled expression.

"And another thing. I don't want you to leave. Please don't go to Denver. Stay here. Stay with me."

"What?" The puzzled expression turned to straight bewilderment.

"Zach, please stay. Let's start again. I'm willing to try if you are."

"Are you sure?"

"I've never been more certain of anything in my life."

He took a step forward and took her hand in his. The heat of his hand sent a spike of warmth surging through her. He searched her face. "What made you change your mind?"

"Part Bree, part Madeline, and part... well, a cardinal."

"A cardinal?"

"It's a long story." She grinned at him.

"Well, we've got time for the story, but first I need to do something." His eyes still searched her face.

"What's that? Are you in pain? Here, let's go inside."

"I'm not in pain." He lifted his hand and brushed his knuckles across her cheek, then gently swept a lock of her hair away from her eyes. "I've never felt better in my whole life."

Her heart soared, just like the cardinal, swooping off into the heavens.

"And another thing." His words were a gentle touch to her soul.

"What's that?" She could barely find her words.

"I think it's about time I told you something." He looked directly into her eyes, and she felt the deepest connection to a human being that she'd ever felt in her life. He continued, "I've fallen in love with you. Probably since the first time I saw you standing there at the chalet with the basket of food. Just took me a while to realize it."

"You *love* me? Are you sure?"

"I've never been more certain of anything in my life." He grinned at her.

She looked up at him. "Remember that wish I made on that star? That night by the lake? When we were sitting on dad's swing?"

"Mm-hmm." He brushed a thumb across her cheek before letting her continue.

"I wished for this."

"This?"

"I wished for someone to love me and look

at me the way you're looking at me right this very minute."

"Ah, Cece. I do love you."

He leaned forward, and she closed her eyes as his lips settled on her once more. Right where they should be.

CHAPTER 25

"You really should pick a wedding date." Cece sat at the table leafing through bridal magazines while Bree looked through a cooking magazine.

"So should you." Bree eyed her over her glasses.

"I'm thinking you should pick October tenth."

"Mom and Dad's anniversary." Bree smiled.

"Right."

"That's such a great idea."

"So great that you want to use the same date?" Bree cocked her head to the side.

"Next year?"

"Nope, this year. Wanna have a double wedding? We'd be inviting the same people. I

know of a great caterer and wedding planner."
Bree grinned.

Cece grinned back. "I guess we should confer with the guys."

"Ha, Jason would marry me tomorrow if I said that's when the wedding was. He's been dying for me to set a date."

"Zach said he wasn't in for a long engagement either." She glanced down at the sparkling solitaire on her finger.

Bree flipped open her computer and went to the calendar for events at the chalet. "It must be meant to be. That weekend is open. Want me to put in our names?"

A wide smile broke across Cece's face. She couldn't think of a better wedding plan than sharing it with her sister. "Put in our names."

ZACH SAT across from Jason in his office. Jason looked up from his computer and grinned at him. "Hey, buddy, guess what?"

"What?"

"It looks like we're getting married."

"You and Bree?"

Jason laughed. "Bree and I and you and

Cece. October tenth." He swiveled the computer around for Zach to see. "Check out the chalet event calendar."

"No kidding?" Zach stared at the online calendar.

Bree Stuart and Jason Cassidy.

Cece Stuart and Zach Berry.

"It's about time those Stuart sisters set a date." He grinned at Jason.

Jason stood, came over, and clapped him on the back. "Looks like we've got a wedding to go to."

"Sure does." Happiness flooded through Zach along with a feeling of excitement. He was going to marry the woman of his dreams. And soon. "Let's go find them."

CHAPTER 26

Bree and Cece stood just outside the doorway leading to the main part of the chalet. It was a perfect fall day. Sunny. The leaves were changing in brilliant shades of autumn splendor. All their friends and family were gathered. Abby had made it in from California, and Madeline and Gil had come back and were staying at the lodge. It seemed like at least half the town had turned out for the wedding.

"I'm just going to peek outside to see if it looks like all the people have gotten inside." Cece turned to open the outside door.

Bree laughed. "Once a wedding planner, always a wedding planner. Even for your own wedding."

Cece grinned. "Hazard of the trade." She opened the door and glanced outside. A bright red cardinal sat on the railing directly in front of her. She stared at it for a moment, and he sang her his song, bobbed his head once, stared at her, then took off in flight, swooping out toward the lake.

It couldn't be the same one…

But she thanked him anyway. For giving her the courage to forgive herself and move on. "Thank you." She whispered the words.

She watched until he disappeared and closed the door softly.

She walked back to her sister and clasped Bree's hand. "Are you ready?"

Bree nodded. "I am."

They turned as Nora walked up to them. "I'm ready, too. Ready to give you both away. An honor that I don't take lightly."

"We couldn't think of anyone we'd rather have do this." Cece smiled at her.

"I'm sure you girls miss your parents, but, I love both of you like daughters." Nora positioned herself between and them took their elbows. The doors swung open wide.

Cece caught her breath at the sight of the

flower-lined aisle and Zach and Jason waiting for them by the arbor.

"You did good, Miss Wedding Planner," Bree whispered.

"*We* did good. With the wedding and these men," Cece whispered back.

The music started, and the Stuart sisters walked down the aisles and into the arms of the men they loved.

NORA SAT in the front row, unashamed of the tears rolling down her face as Jason kissed Bree. What a year it had been, but both her children were married now, and she couldn't be more delighted.

Annie leaned against her shoulder. "I've never seen Jason look happier."

"All four of them look happy, don't they?"

Annie nodded and smiled.

Nora looked around the chalet, ecstatic that it was finished and her son could have such a wonderful venue to get married in. The chalet had turned out so nice, and they had it booked for so many weekends stretching out into the future. As usual, Jason had made a good business decision with suggesting they add the chalet as a wedding and meeting venue. She was so grateful that he'd joined her in running the lodge. And Bree and Cece's business was doing well, too. Life was just pretty darn perfect right now.

"You're a very lucky Momma," Annie whispered.

"That I am." Her heart swelled with happiness and contentment. Enough happiness and contentment to go around for everyone.

Annie squeezed her hand as they watched Jason and Bree and Cece and Zach walk back down the aisle, married couples with radiant smiles on their faces.

She wanted for nothing and had everything she'd ever dreamed of.

Everything was just perfect in Sweet River Falls today. Everything.

DEAR READER,

I know, I know… you're wanting Nora's story, right? Don't worry, it will be out in early Fall of 2019. Until then, did you miss THE LETTER in the Comfort Crossing series with

Madeline and Gil's story? You can get it here at your favorite retailer:

The Letter - Book Three in the Comfort Crossing Series

Or try out another one of my series:

Book One in the Lighthouse Point series:

Wish Upon a Shell

Book One in the Comfort Crossing series:

The Shop on Main

As always, I appreciate each and every one of you. Happy reading!

Kay

THANK YOU for reading my story. I hope you enjoyed it. Sign up for my newsletter to be updated with information on new releases, promotions, give-aways, and newsletter-only surprises. The signup is at my website, kaycorrell.com.

Reviews help other readers find new books. I always appreciate when my readers take time to leave an honest review.

I love to hear from my readers. Feel free to contact me at authorcontact@kaycorrell.com

COMFORT CROSSING ~ THE SERIES

The Shop on Main - Book One

The Memory Box - Book Two

The Christmas Cottage - A Holiday Novella (Book 2.5)

The Letter - Book Three

The Christmas Scarf - A Holiday Novella (Book 3.5)

The Magnolia Cafe - Book Four

The Unexpected Wedding - Book Five

The Wedding in the Grove (crossover short story between series - Josephine and Paul from The Letter.)

LIGHTHOUSE POINT ~ THE SERIES

Wish Upon a Shell - Book One

Wedding on the Beach - Book Two

Love at the Lighthouse - Book Three

Cottage near the Point - Book Four

Return to the Island - Book Five

Bungalow by the Bay - Book Six

SWEET RIVER ~ THE SERIES

A Dream to Believe in - Book One

A Memory to Cherish - Book Two

A Song to Remember - Book Three

A Time to Forgive - Book Four

A Summer of Secrets - Book Five

INDIGO BAY ~ a multi-author series of sweet romance

Sweet Sunrise - Book Three

Sweet Holiday Memories - A short holiday story

Sweet Starlight - Book Nine

ABOUT THE AUTHOR

Kay writes sweet, heartwarming stories that are a cross between women's fiction and contemporary romance. She is known for her charming small towns, quirky townsfolk, and enduring strong friendships between the women in her books.

Kay lives in the Midwest of the U.S. and can often be found out and about with her camera, taking a myriad of photographs which she likes to incorporate into her book covers. When not lost in her writing or photography, she can be found spending time with her ever-supportive husband, knitting, or playing with her puppies —two cavaliers and one naughty but adorable Australian shepherd. Kay and her husband also love to travel. When it comes to vacation time, she is torn between a nice trip to the beach or the mountains—but the mountains only get considered in the summer—she swears she's allergic to snow.

Learn more about Kay and her books at kaycorrell.com

While you're there, sign up for her newsletter to hear about new releases, sales, and giveaways.

WHERE TO FIND ME:
kaycorrell.com
authorcontact@kaycorrell.com

Join my Facebook Reader Group. We have lots of fun and you'll hear about sales and new releases first!
https://www.facebook.com/groups/KayCorrell/

facebook.com/KayCorrellAuthor

instagram.com/kaycorrell

pinterest.com/kaycorrellauthor

amazon.com/author/kaycorrell

bookbub.com/authors/kay-correll